From *Bad Boy Billionaire's Lady*

Elizabeth struggled against Skullcap's hold, impotently, horrified that the situation had careened so out of control. Her blood thundered in her ears as she tried desperately to think of a way out...or was that the sound of a motor?

Suddenly, the hard roar of a powerful machine filled the mouth of the alley.

Beyond the muggers, a motorcycle skidded into the narrow way, its harsh engine reverberating against the buildings.

The goon spun toward the intruder. Freed, Elizabeth clutched the carrier and stumbled back, her pulse racing frantically.

The bike tore down the pavement and squealed to a stop a few feet from the mugger.

A big, helmeted, leather-clad man sat easily on the low-slung seat. Scuffed, shitkicker boots rested flat on the pavement.

Her panted breaths rasped in her ears. The mugger's more dangerous biker pal? God, and she'd thought things couldn't get worse.

One boot rose to toe the stand down. With a fluid lift of his muscular leg, the man dismounted easily, unfolding to almost a giant's height. Face completely covered by a mirrored visor, he stood before them without a word.

More dangerous? Try deadly.

Elizabeth's breath came in frosted little pants. Was she rescued, or in even more trouble than before?

Bad Boy Billionaire's Lady

The Lovless Billionaires. Three brothers with too much money and no time for love—until each meets the woman guaranteed to infuriate—and inflame—him most.

Rebel Lovless ran away from home to escape his robber-baron grandfather molding him into a ruthless copy. But when the old man dies, Reb, now a Navy SEAL, must return to take over the conglomerate.

Elizabeth Rothschild promised a dying man she'd protect his charitable legacy. But how, when the greedy, manipulative sharks on the board want her out?

And now the biggest shark of all, the Lovless heir, is coming home.

The loner and out-of-sync boy who left is not the stunning man who strides into the board meeting. He shocks them all by barking orders and commanding them to a team-building exercise on a tropical island. They're getting their hands dirty constructing a house. But as Reb, Elizabeth, and the board members toil side by side, will it build their camaraderie—or only put them close enough for someone to stick in the knife?

Look for these titles by Mary Hughes

Now Available:

Romantic Adventure
Edie and the CEO—Crimson Romance
Falling ~~on~~ for the Billionaire
Cin Wikkid: April Fools For Love
Hot Chips and Sand
Bad Boy Billionaire's Lady: Lovless Brothers
Playing With Fire: The Battle of the Bands

Biting Love/The Ancients
Bite My Fire—Entangled
Biting Nixie—Entangled
The Bite of Silence—Entangled
Biting Me Softly—Entangled
Biting Oz—Entangled
Beauty Bites—Entangled
Downbeat—Entangled
Assassins Bite—Entangled
Passion Bites—Entangled
Biting Love Nibbles
Night's Caress

Pull of the Moon Series
Prophecy Mates
Heart Mates
Hunt Mates
Mind Mates

Standalone
Black Diamond Jinn

Coming Soon:

The Classic Billionaire's Newshound (Lovless Brothers)
The Genius Billionaire's Hacker (Lovless Brothers)
Night's Kiss (The Ancients)
Night's Bliss (The Ancients)
Soul Mates (Pull of the Moon)

Bad Boy Billionaire's Lady
Lovless Brothers

Mary Hughes

DEDICATION

To Gregg, for making me carrot cake with cream cheese frosting—and all the love that goes along with it.

My profound thanks to Stacy D. Holmes for her superlative editing and Scott Carpenter for another beautiful cover.

Chapter One

The trouble started when Elizabeth Rothschild, toting the rescue kitten, tried to dodge New York City rush-hour foot traffic by cutting through a dark alley.

She was late for an important after-hours board meeting. Stopping at the animal shelter to see if they needed food or medicine—part of her job as head of charities for Lovless Industries, but also her passion—made her later.

The kitten had been mewing piteously. She'd picked it up to cuddle and console it. Big eyes blinked trustingly at her from the ball of yellow fur, and she was lost, plucking the stray from the shelter to give him a home.

Now, as she muddled along the congested sidewalk, she kept one arm securely around the kitten's tote. Her messenger bag flopped against her other hip, its strap crisscrossed with the carrier. Taking the poor animal with her probably wasn't her best idea, but there'd been no time. A friend at work could watch the kitten during her meeting.

Jostled and late, the empty alley looked like salvation.

She ducked out of the press of bodies into the alley opening. Clutching the carrier, she peered down the dark, narrow path between the two tall buildings.

Deserted? Or hiding dangers?

She touched her knit hat. Her hair was safe from grabbing underneath. Muggings were no joke, but her coat covered her expensive power suit and nice jewelry. And she wore a good pair of runners.

One arm still around the kitten's carrier, she dug with the other hand in her messenger bag for her phone and checked the time.

Five minutes until the meeting. And she still had to find her friend to drop off the little ball of fur.

Elizabeth swore. Walk in late? Or potentially not at all? She shifted on her runners, thinking of the boardroom that awaited, the big table ringed by two dozen of the greediest, most blood-thirsty suited sharks there were—and no more Landy to support her.

"One goal," she coached herself. "Protect Landy's charity legacy. Well, and not get fired."

The kitten, perhaps hearing her voice, meowed.

"Okay, three goals," she answered. "Protect the charities, don't get fired, and buy you kitten chow. But for now, don't worry. Ainsley will take good care of you while I face the sharks."

The sharks, and one other complication—the new chairman of the Lovless Industries board of directors. A man even Landy called uncontrollable. Her stomach lurched, remembering her mentor's last words to her.

"You'll have to deal with my grandson."

Muggers or sharks? *Oh, what's the difference?*

"Right." She made her decision.

*   *   *

The man saddled with the appalling name of "Landon Lovless the Third" was pissed.

The snarl of traffic, beeping and honking around him, echoed his mood. He sat on his motorcycle amid New York rush hour, hot and chafing despite the cool day. He ought to be with his SEAL team, not dressed up in this ridiculous suit. He ought to be hearing his brothers in arms calling him Rebel and Reb instead of a pack of corporate wolves calling him Landon or Lovless or worse yet, Mr. Chairman.

That was his old robber baron of a grandfather, not him.

Yet everything he'd rejected from day one, the name, the title, the money, had been forced on him by the old man's death.

"I won't do it," Reb snarled for the umpteenth time. He'd donned his leathers over the suit and rode his Harley through midtown rush hour traffic in protest. It made him late, but that was a form of protest, too.

The light changed. Cars, cabs, and bikes moved forward. He rolled on the throttle—clamping and stomping the brakes when, three inches later, the car in front of him squealed to a halt. Clamping the bike into neutral, he slapped boots to the pavement. The left lane was supposed to be faster, but nothing moved right now. He was hot and late, and the fact that he'd done it to himself made him even more pissed.

Then he saw her.

Immediately, everything else dropped away, including his temper. He didn't know what about her attracted his attention; she scurried into his periphery, about a block behind him on the sidewalk, nothing out of the ordinary.

Her lumpy cloche hat looked hand-knit—like something made by a kid, not the trendy, artisanal kind his grandfather's too-young mistresses wore. Her coat appeared to be good quality wool, but a bit scuffed looking.

His forehead tightened in a frown beneath his helmet. Everything she wore looked a little worn, including her no-name running shoes and the messenger bag where, if she was like every other New York City office worker he'd met, she'd tote her sensible pumps. Unless she was the back-killing heels type.

The pet carrier looked new, though.

Then her face came into focus. *She* wasn't worn-looking at all. As she hurried nearer, he was struck by her creamy skin, sparkling eyes, and ruby lips perfect for a man's kiss...

He shook his head and turned away. Then turned almost immediately back.

Little wisps of blonde hair escaped from her hat. He normally couldn't stand blondes, but something about those small, fragile curls, shimmering silver and honey and flaxen, intrigued him as she scurried past him on the sidewalk.

As she neared the alley and slowed.

Damn it. He could almost hear the thought going through her head.

Don't do it.

Ignoring his mental warnings—and plain good sense—she swiveled on graceful legs and went into the alley.

The dark alley.

He chomped molars and turned away. Not his problem. She'd done it of her own free will. On her own head be it.

That dark, narrow alley. Perfect for an enemy ambush.

He glanced again at the shadowed maw. Nothing good came of pretty women cutting through alleys.

Forcing himself to look away, he told himself it was none of his business. Besides, he'd have to cut across two lanes plus the congested sidewalk...

She might be in danger, the SEAL in him urged.

The light changed. Traffic began flowing forward.

He eased out the clutch, first gear engaged, and rolled forward with traffic. *She made the choice herself—*

The panicked yowl of a young animal caught his ears.

Barely audible over the traffic noise. But his hearing, attuned to danger, meant the poor beast's fear cut through.

With a sharp curse, he cranked his fork. Earning several honks and rude gestures, he shoved the bike into non-existent gaps in the wall-to-wall traffic. He only hoped he wasn't too late.

*   *   *

As Elizabeth hurried down the alley, a big, bulky man stepped from a shadowed doorway to block her path.

"Where're you going so fast?"

Her blood iced. The man was all beef and flexing muscle, with flinty eyes. She clasped the kitten's carrier to her, forcing herself to breathe deeply, trying to slow her heart's pounding in her ribcage. She knew what to do— extract her wallet from her messenger bag, toss it behind the guy, and while he was distracted snatching it up, run the other way.

A clattering from behind caught her attention. She glanced over her shoulder as a second goon slouched into the alley. His knit cap hugged his skull, the hat's brim rolled to expose his hungry eyes.

Skullcap had just cut off her escape route.

She swallowed, hard. Squaring her shoulders, she faced the first mugger and thrust out a palm. "Back off."

Instead, the beefy man sauntered closer. "What's in the carrier?"

Her arm convulsed around the animal tote. A worried meow answered. "A cat. You don't want him. You want my briefcase. You can have it." She eased the messenger bag from her shoulder. "Just a bunch of work papers, though. A subway pass. Credit cards, but they're maxed out." And her phone and second-hand Gucci pumps, which she'd counted on to make the right impression with the new chairman.

But the best way out of the situation was to give the mugger the bag.

She glanced behind again, wondering if she could toss it far enough to have both muggers run after it, when the beefy man suddenly grabbed the strap.

She automatically yanked it away. Her fear and fury and rampaging adrenaline boosted the tug into a full-body swing. She spun around—and whirled the bag into the beefy man's head.

"Hey!" He threw up a hand last-minute, but she still managed to wallop him in the skull. He collapsed with a groan to his hands and knees.

Her jaw dropped in amazement. Then self-preservation kicked in, and she lurched into a run past him. One step, two, she built up speed, her gaze zeroed on the street opening at the other end of the alley.

Just let me escape. I vow never to take a shortcut again.

Feet pursued her. A hand clamped onto her coat. Her pulse kicked into overdrive.

"Where d'you think you're going?" Skullcap dragged her to a stop.

She swung around, messenger bag first, the kitten still clamped to her body.

Skullcap caught the briefcase mid-swing, ripped it from her grasp, and threw it to one side.

"Bad move, bitch." He slapped her face.

His palm was like a flat rock smashing into her cheek. Her bone rang with the impact, and her head spun with the momentum, jarring her off balance. She stumbled back a step. The pain came an instant later, sharp, insistent. She willed it down to a dull throb, desperately trying to keep control of what she could.

The mugger grabbed her by the lapels—and tore open her coat beneath the carrier strap.

She sucked in a shocked breath. Inhaled a wash of male stink. She recoiled automatically, heart hammering. The kitten released a terrified screech.

"Well, well." The mugger dragged her back, his foul excitement pouring off him. "What's this?"

Beyond him, the beefy man was just rising. "Hold her." Hand to his head where she'd clipped him, he staggered toward her. "I owe her some payback."

She struggled against Skullcap's hold, impotently, horrified that the situation had careened so out of control. Her blood thundered in her ears as she tried desperately to think of a way out...or was that the sound of a motor?

Suddenly, the hard roar of a powerful machine filled the mouth of the alley.

Beyond the muggers, a motorcycle skidded into the narrow way, its harsh engine reverberating against the buildings.

Both goons spun toward the intruder. Freed, Elizabeth clutched the carrier and stumbled back, her pulse racing frantically.

The bike tore down the pavement and squealed to a stop a few feet from the muggers.

A big, helmeted, leather-clad man sat easily on the low-slung seat. Scuffed, shitkicker boots rested flat on the pavement.

Her panted breaths rasped in her ears. The muggers' more dangerous biker pal? God, and she'd thought things couldn't get worse.

One boot rose to toe the stand down. With a fluid lift of his muscular leg, the man dismounted easily, unfolding to almost a giant's height. Face completely covered by a mirrored visor, he stood before them without a word.

More dangerous? Try deadly.

Elizabeth's breath came in frosted little pants. Was she rescued, or in even more trouble than before?

Chapter Two

Arms wrapped protectively around the kitten carrier, Elizabeth couldn't decide if she should run or stay. Her feet decided for her, shuffling her backward.

The big biker simply stood there at his ease as the pair of muggers approached him. From their aggressive, almost threatening stalks, she took back the thought they might have been friends.

But if the biker was here to rescue her, it was two against one. She had to do something.

Call for help. Right.

Except her phone was in her messenger bag, lying where her attacker had thrown it to one side, fetched up against a building. She edged toward the bag—just as the beefy mugger launched a sledgehammer fist at the biker's gut.

Her breath stuck in her throat.

The man simply pivoted, and the mugger's fist swished harmlessly past his jacket. As the thug's arm extended, the biker's leather-clad one wrapped around it. Continuing the pivot, he used the mugger's momentum to send him flying over one hip.

It didn't even look like he had to work too hard.

The beefy goon landed on his backside with an *oof.* Elizabeth gave a mental cheer—until he pushed himself to his feet, grinned savagely at the biker, and drew a knife.

Phone! Throwing aside subtlety, she darted toward her messenger bag.

"Hey!" Skullcap pulled his own knife and moved to intercept her.

Panic goosed her into a mad dash. *Nearly there.* She elbowed the cat carrier behind her as she reached for the bag...

A hand clamped her arm. Her heart nearly leaped from her chest.

"Gotcha now."

"*Leave her alone,*" the biker ripped out like a chainsaw. He spun a kick through the beefy mugger's head and without even waiting for the reeling man to fall, ran toward them.

Skullcap yanked her against him, brandishing his knife at the man. "Stop!"

The kitten shrieked. The poor animal's distress turned Elizabeth's fear to fury, burning fiercely through her.

She kicked hard at the side of the mugger's knee.

Bleating in surprise, the thug stumbled sideways, his hand automatically releasing her just as the biker reached them.

He caught Skullcap's knife-hand wrist and yanked him down—into his own raised, leather-clad knee. Mugger nose met biker bone. The knife clattered to the pavement.

Skullcap sprang back with a shriek, hand to his bloody face. Fury lit his eyes. "You asshole!" He charged.

The biker spun. Lightning fast, that shitkicker boot planted in mugger belly. The kick lifted Skullcap from the concrete and sent him flying. He butt-planted a few feet away, collapsing flat with a moan.

"Damn it." The beefy mugger shook his head, rose, and staggered almost drunkenly toward them. Her leather-clad rescuer took two strides to him, laced his gloved fists together—and hammered the mugger in the skull.

The beefy man fell back to the ground with a pained sigh.

Her heart hammered five painful beats before she realized it was actually over. Body pulsing with leftover shock, she fought to calm herself—her composure broken instantly when that black helmet swiveled to face her.

She swallowed a dry gulp and managed to stutter, "Th-thank you. You saved me..."

Light flared off the polycarbonate, hitting her like a glare—except for a single swatch of matte black just above the visor. An eagle-and-trident appliqué.

Without a word, the man spun and stalked to his bike. He mounted, started the beast, and roared past her, disappearing out the alley on the other side.

Elizabeth stared after him, not sure what to think. She'd been scared out of her wits, but then a hero roared up and rescued her—and took off without a word.

Touching her fingers to breastbone, she felt the excited thud of her heart. She usually did the protecting, the rescuing, doubly hard as a woman in a male-dominated world. Was that why she was so impressed? She was honored to protect Landy's charities, but being strong all the time took its toll.

The kitten mewed.

Well, one thing was sure. She needed to get the poor creature somewhere with water and papers. She snatched up her messenger bag.

Following the biker's path toward the end of the alley, she clasped the carrier close under one arm, her messenger back under the other, and jogged out.

*   *   *

"I need your help," Elizabeth belted out as she scurried past Ainsley into her tiny office. Setting the cat carrier gently in one corner, she threw off her coat and hat, dumped her messenger bag onto her chair, and dug inside for her good heels.

Her friend and roommate trotted in behind her. Like a radical protester from the nineteen-sixties, Ainsley had straight, long brown hair parted in the middle and falling around her high cheekbones and heart-shaped face. But she was a radical reporter for an online exposé journal, fully in this century. Elizabeth had helped her get this temporary job at Lovless Industries writing technical copy.

Curiosity lighting her elfin face, Ainsley went straight to the carrier. "Is that a cat?"

"Kitten." Setting her Gucci pumps on the ground, Elizabeth toed off her runners then slid her feet into the heels. Stepping into the cool leather, she felt her stature rise, giving her a much-needed boost to her confidence. "Can you watch him while I brave the board?"

"Of course. What's his name?"

"I haven't decided." What else? Oh yes, her phone.

"How about Meowster Furry-purry?"

She'd have winced, but she was too rushed. "Whimsical, but impractical." Retrieving her phone from her bag, she tucked it into her skirt pocket.

"Sugar Lumps?"

"Um...maybe wait until I get back? Thanks for watching him."

Leaving the kitten with her friend, hoping desperately that Ainsley wouldn't be cooing Cutie Pie at him by the time she returned, Elizabeth rushed out, headed for the boardroom.

Ding. A text message.

She slid the wafer-thin device from her pocket and thumbed up the message.

Preston Hare, her only ally on the board. —*Yr late.*—

"Tell me something I don't know," she muttered, jamming the phone back in her pocket as the boardroom came into sight.

Her heart thudded harder. Ten-foot-tall slabs of solid oak with *Lovless Industries* inlaid in jade, the double doors were meant to be imposing. Tonight, they were downright intimidating.

Another ding stopped her outside the monoliths. With a soft snarl, she pulled out the phone.

—*Dont mk me regret helpng u.*—

Her only ally? In truth, Preston Hare—which he pronounced Hah-ree, like Mata Hari—was as sharky as the rest of the board.

He was also her ex-boyfriend. After their breakup, she chose to use the more-obvious pronunciation of his last name....with an added "Ball."

The enemy of my enemy is my friend, she reminded herself. *You promised Landy you'd save his charities, and you can't do that without Preston.*

Smoothing a hand along her hair, she patted strands disheveled by the attack into place, patting her emotions into place with them. Then, with a deep breath for courage, she pushed one of the massive doors open, having to put her shoulder into the effort. She'd have resented it, but if she resented all the things here that were skewed toward men, she'd be a seething cauldron of anger.

Gazes around the table rose to her, glaring, disdainful, hitting her right in the confidence bone.

She hesitated.

Mistake. Almost as one the men ringing the table smiled. Not in welcome, but the smiles of sharks scenting blood. *Her* blood.

Landy would've cut them down to size with an ice-blue glare. *Landy isn't here.*

Elizabeth nerved herself to enter despite their rapacious smiles. She took one step forward—and her heel wobbled under her.

The grins widened. *Another step closer to being ousted.*

She righted herself. Pretending a confidence she didn't feel, she made her way toward Preston, glancing at faces as she passed. There were three distinct types of shark—the middle-aged hatchet men, the lean, hungry up-and-comers, and the silver-haired old guard. *You're too soft,* one hatchet face said. *Charities make no profit,* a young buck glared. *A woman,* scoffed an old silverback's sneer.

Roland Exetor Senior, worst of the old guard, glared at her from pockets of flesh. "Elizabeth. You're late." He sat mid-table, though not in Landy's old seat.

No, across from Senior, one of the hatchet men sat smugly in the big leather command chair.

Suddenly fed up with it all, she snapped, "I was nearly mugged. Thanks for asking." She stomped past the old guard and hatchet men to the only open chair, beside Preston at the young-buck end.

As she sat, she scanned the rest of the faces, looking for Landy's grandson. The boy was only a set of old snapshots and Landy's hissed complaints to her. The boardroom held no sullen, lanky teen, no wiry, strung-out wreck with Landy's eyes.

He wasn't here yet. *At least I'm not the only one late.*

Preston slapped the table. "Can we get back to my concerns? The heir not being here yet is a bad sign."

"What a fuck-up," Exetor Senior muttered

"I knew his father," one of the hatchet men said. "Lovless Junior ran away from responsibility. The grandson is worse."

"A fuck-up," Exetor Senior repeated. "Always rejecting his grandfather's good advice."

"Exactly my point." Preston jabbed a finger onto the table in percussive emphasis. "As *we* need to reject *him*."

She remembered Preston phoning her right after Landy died. *"The board has always wanted you out, Elizabeth. Now's their chance, unless..."*

"Unless what?"

"Unless I become chairman in the old man's place."

"What about the Lovless heir?"

"We get rid of him. C'mon, Elizabeth. You support me, I'll support you."

That was the scheme she and Preston had devised. Oust the heir and make Preston chairman. *It's my best opportunity to help Landy's charities survive.*

"Vote Lovless out before he even arrives?" The young shark across from Preston grinned. "I like."

Roland Exetor Junior, or as she liked to call him, Rolex. He was the epitome of modern shark in a gray patterned skinny suit, white power tie, and capped grin that didn't soften, or even reach, his eyes. He was the greediest, most ruthless of them all, blaming her for Landy's softening of heart. He hated her for it.

But he hated the heir more. Rolex *would* have been Landy's heir apparent, if not for the Lovless prodigal son.

Or rather, prodigal grandson—Landon Lovless III.

"Have some subtlety, boy." Exetor Senior chuckled. "We'll get him out, all right, but by guile. He'll never know it wasn't his own idea."

Elizabeth's breath chilled. Was the old silverback one step ahead of her and Preston?

She glanced at her ex. He wouldn't look at her.

Her mouth dried. Why wouldn't Preston meet her gaze? Did he know something she didn't? She half-expected to get axed, but did they mean to do it tonight? Without the heir's blessing?

Before I can get Preston elected in his place?

She wished Landy were here. He knew what went on in the sharks' minds and hearts—he'd been just like them, once.

"Why hold back?" Rolex asked his father, tone slightly petulant. "Our previous chairman wouldn't have. He was merciless."

Landy had to be, to hack and slash Lovless Industries from a single mining company to today's powerhouse conglomerate.

"We're more refined now, my boy." Senior was as condescending with his own son as he was to Elizabeth. "As befits our new place in the world." With subsidiaries in everything from transportation to food prep, LI's largest moneymakers were mining, refining, and recycling rare earth materials. Computer materials. Idea materials.

"Can we get started?" one of Senior's cronies grumbled. "I'll miss my dinner engagement."

"We've waited for the fuck-up long enough," Rolex sneered.

"It *will* throw him." Exetor Senior nodded. "Let's get started—"

Boom. The doors exploded open, flung apart as if they weighed nothing by a tall man in a perfectly cut suit. The action pulled apart the lapels to reveal acres of crisp, sky-colored shirt over a powerful chest.

The sharks eyed the newcomer. It was obvious from their smirks they still saw the sullen loner.

Heart pounding faster, Elizabeth wasn't so sure.

Landon Lovless III, with black hair, blue eyes so brilliant they were silver, and a face that was all dark, dangerous planes might be the biggest shark in the tank.

Chapter Three

Lovless released the doors and stalked into the room, his stride like a lion, staking out its territory.

Elizabeth barely stopped herself from fluttering a hand to her breast. The sharks would've torn her apart for sure—as an appetizer for their feeding frenzy on the newcomer.

The hatchet men sat straighter, ready to attack. The young bucks, sensing easy prey, pawed to maul what was left.

The heir stopped. Exetor Senior's grin grew. Elizabeth knew why. Though the table comfortably seated the whole board and then some, she'd taken the last chair in the room. Senior must've arranged for the rest to be removed.

With all the seats filled, Lovless would have to leave to find a chair, bring it back, and try to wedge it in somewhere, all spoiling that powerful entrance. A deliberate ploy to put the heir on the defensive. Elizabeth wondered if Preston had come up with it.

But Lovless simply stalked to the biggest chair, mid-table—the seat that would've been Landy's. He stood there, tall and menacing, and stared down at the unfortunate hatchet man in that chair.

The man pretended to ignore him, but he tugged a bit at his collar.

Lovless' silver eyes narrowed. His gaze was so concentrated Elizabeth was surprised that, like a magnifying glass on a sunny day, the man's hair didn't start on fire.

The hatchet man began squirming.

The heir cleared his throat. Pointedly.

The hatchet man shot an apologetic glance at Preston. It *was* her ex's maneuver. The man scuffed back the chair, rose, and slunk out of the room.

Lovless, however, didn't drop into the vacated chair. No, he stood there, silent. Making everyone in the room wait. The old-fashioned clock in the corner ticked away in the hush. The heir had turned the table on the old goats, making them uncomfortable instead.

Bravo, Elizabeth thought. Yes, she wanted him out in favor of Preston, but she had to admire what he'd done. In one, wordless coup, he'd leveled the playing field.

The hatchet man returned, wrestling a big chair through the heavy door. He dragged it, scudding against the carpet, to where Preston sat. Her ex wouldn't move. With a thwarted growl, the man shoved his chair in beside Elizabeth—actually, nearly on top of her, in a blatant display of territorial dominance.

She only snorted, scooting her chair over. The guy'd been kicked by the boss and was passing it down. She could kick him back, but why? He'd already been handily defeated.

The heir stood there the whole time. Silver eyes narrow, black head haloed by the setting red sun until most of them had to blink back tears to see him. Then he simply pulled out his chair and sat. "Let's get started."

Exetor Senior cleared his throat. "Yes. Finally. The agenda on the table—"

"Is scrapped," Lovless snapped. "I've reviewed board minutes, company metrics, and financials, and frankly, lady and gentlemen, I'm appalled."

Senior harrumphed. "Now, see here, Landon—"

"Client satisfaction, down. New orders, down. Profits, down." His silver stare cut to the older man. "These are not trivial complaints, *Rolly*."

Senior's grimace told Elizabeth the heir had scored a hit on the old shark.

Lovless continued, "I never wanted anything to do with Lovless Industries. I'd intended to step down as chairperson—"

"A good idea," the hatchet man beside her interjected. "No MBA, never attended any board meetings—*frankly*, you don't have the background to handle trillion-dollar assets."

"What Mr. Rams means to say is that we're here to help you." Exetor Senior smirked. "Let the professionals handle the boring day-to-day chores. You just lean back and reap the benefits..."

The old man dribbled off because Lovless had simply placed two fists precisely on the table, risen slightly, and leaned forward, his chest muscles swelling beneath his shirt.

"I *was* going to step aside. But *frankly*"—he slashed a glare at the hatchet man—"seeing these terrible numbers, I can't." He sat again.

Elizabeth watched him in awe. They'd tried to twist him around, but he'd barked at them like a drill sergeant, stripping them to raw recruits. She'd have applauded, but her own plans to put Preston in as chairman also began to crumble, churning worry into her gut.

Exetor Senior tut-tutted. "You're overreacting, my boy. The nuances of a general ledger are hard enough for an MBA to understand, much less a high-school dropout."

Ouch. No worse than Landy's tirades about his grandson, but Elizabeth winced on the heir's behalf.

"So, let's just adjourn this meeting." Senior smiled benevolently and went in for the kill. "You can come to my office, and I'm sure if I just explain the reports to you—"

"Old man, those numbers would've been plain to a kindergartener." Lovless grinned his own sharp, white smile. "And here is a number even you should understand—fifty-one percent. That's the share of this conglomerate owned by myself and my brothers. So here's what we're going to do. This board needs to go back to basics. Teamwork. You will all accompany me to Haight Island in the Caribbean for intensive teambuilding exercises."

"A spa?" Senior snorted. "I can get a massage here. And it will have a happier ending."

"Hardly. The Lovless Resort is there—but we'll be working in the village." Lovless' grin was all shark. "Less massage, more Army basic training."

Shocked silence greeted that statement. Then they all started blabbering at once.

"I don't have time for nonsense."

"Training camp? At my age?"

"Who does he think he is?"

Rolex rapped the table for everyone's attention. "What about Elizabeth?" he challenged the heir. "If we're roughing it, she won't want to come."

She winced. Here it was, the moment of truth. Competing in a man's world, she had to be tougher than tough. But Army basic training? She could swim competently enough, but the thought of running miles, scaling rough timber walls, and being yelled at 24/7...she *could,* but she didn't want to.

Still, she said bravely, "Anything you can do, Roland, I can do."

"Really?" he sneered. "Can you bench press two hundred pounds? Can you run a marathon?" Rolex pounded home his point. "Can you run at all in those shoes?"

Damn it. Now Lovless would exclude her. Cut her out of any wheeling and dealing done on the island. It was only a few steps from that to being eased out altogether.

And she'd be forced to renege on a promise made to a dying old man.

No, she'd find some way to protect Landy's charities. It would just be a lot harder.

Then Lovless snapped, "This isn't just about brawn."

"Brains, then," Rolex said. "Constitution. Men are smarter and tougher. It's just fact."

"You're an ass if you think that." The heir's silver eyes sparked. "And you've exactly proved my point—you're dividing the group instead of pulling together. Which is pretty dumb. This retreat is about teamwork. And Ms. Rothschild will most certainly be part of the team."

She gaped. He'd actually defended her? She'd have been surprised he knew her name, but he'd already proved he'd studied both board and conglomerate like a general.

"We leave first thing tomorrow. The climate is humid and hot, and the work is hard, but there's that five-star resort. Pack accordingly. We'll be there one week. At the end of that time, we'll have another board meeting. If it isn't markedly different from what I see now…"

He left the consequences unnamed, but Elizabeth thought no Ghost of Christmas Past could be scarier than Lovless right now.

"You." Rising, he pointed at Rolex. "And you." He pointed at Elizabeth.

Her stomach dropped.

"Come with me." He swept out of the room.

Chapter Four

"Damn it. That didn't go the way we expected." Roland Exetor Junior shot to his feet and, after exchanging a frustrated glare with his father, stalked out after Lovless.

Elizabeth pushed back her chair, her gut churning. Landy's heir had defended her right to come along on the teambuilding retreat. But now he wanted to see her and her biggest detractor?

Alone?

With a deep breath for courage, she rose to follow.

Preston's hand closed around her arm, stopping her. "Get him on our side," he hissed.

She'd figured that out early on, so she only nodded.

"Any way you have to. Any. Way." He added a mouthed, *The oldest way.*

He meant sex.

Ewww.

Not because of Lovless. The man was tall, well-built, and good-looking. But sex to curry favor? Definitely not.

"I'm sure that won't be necessary." She shook off her ex's hand and stalked out of the boardroom. Typical

Preston. When he got a goal in his sights, no price was too high—especially if paid by someone else. *Jerk.*

Walking the short corridor to Landy's corner office suite brought back a slew of memories. She'd spent so many hours with the old man, arguing over his various charitable organizations. The youth music program, the junior astronaut training for disadvantaged children, the animal shelter...which reminded her she needed to get the kitten home and situated as soon as possible.

She paused at the doorway. Deep breath, and enter.

Her memory had already painted Landy's gray, bent frame behind the desk, swallowed by his huge executive chair. So the tall, straight, broad-shouldered form of the Lovless heir filling the seat shocked her. Saddened her.

A momentary shimmering welled in her eyes.

"Don't take all day, Elizabeth," Rolex spat testily, sounding like his old man.

With a sigh, she headed for the smaller of two guest chairs, Rolex having already nabbed the larger.

The power play grated. As she slid into her chair, she reminded herself it might not be a power play. His frame was slightly bigger than hers.

Probably a power play, though.

Through all this, Landon Lovless III sat silently, hands folded comfortably before him on the desk. His broad shoulders were accentuated by his costly tailored suit, his extensive chest was barely civilized by his crisp shirt and understated, rich silk tie, and his face was hewn from hardest granite by a master.

Preston's *"Any. Way."* echoed in her mind. Bedding this man would definitely not be a chore. Wrong, but not hard.

He dominated the space like he owned it, even though not a thing had changed in the office, not even the big decorative name plate/pen set, proudly declaring *Landon Lovless Senior.* She glanced around, frowning thoughtfully. Why hadn't the heir obliterated his grandfather's presence? Rolex would have.

"This is insane." The younger Exetor broke the silence. "A third of those men are old enough to be your father. Another third are old enough to be your grandfather. How can you possibly think to run them over an obstacle course or put them through a bunch of stupid trust exercises or whatever madness you have in mind? They'll be dead of a heart attack or having strokes before they reach the finish line." He thumped the desk with a knuckle. "Or is that *really* what you want? To kill off your competition?"

Lovless sat still through the entire tirade. Elizabeth wondered and worried a bit at that, until she saw it wasn't the stillness of befuddlement or even acceptance.

It was the patient waiting of a predator for the prey to tire.

Sure enough, as Rolex ran out of steam, the heir gave a quick, sharp, white grin.

Here it comes.

"You're right. *If* I was planning on obstacle courses and exercises, I'd need straightening out, pronto. Congratulations, you've just proved I made the right choice."

"Choice?" Rolex sputtered. "Choice for what?"

"Every commander needs a left and right hand. That's you two."

Elizabeth's jaw dropped.

"The right hand works for me," Lovless went on. "And the left hand—"

"Works against you?" Rolex sneered.

"Traditionally, he thinks like the enemy. Shows me the flaws in my plans."

"I'm nobody's left hand."

"You are. You just proved it yourself. But if you want me to choose another confidant..."

He left it hanging, but the implications were clear. *Join me, or I'll promote someone else.*

Muttering, Rolex rose from the chair and stalked to the doorway with righteous indignation.

Twisting in her chair, she followed him from the corner of her eye. She was impressed and a little frightened at how fast, how *easily* the heir had taken command. He'd bent all these big tough sharks to his will. He'd even coerced Rolex into doing what he wanted.

How easily could the man break her?

The office was large enough that by the time Rolex got to the door, his stalk looked more like a sullen stomp. But as he opened the door, he turned with a malicious grin.

Elizabeth could see the corporate gamesmanship going on behind his eyes.

His mouth opened to deliver a parting line—scathing, with no rebuttal possible, because he'd disappear the instant he'd scored the hit.

She'd been victim of that gamesmanship more than once.

Her protective instincts rose. Scary, bigger shark or not, Lovless didn't deserve Rolex's power play.

As he drew breath for his parting shot, she turned her back on him. "Mr. Lovless, before Mr. Exetor goes to prepare—what time are we leaving tomorrow?"

One corner of those chiseled lips lifted in a knowing smile. He'd seen, and understood, what she'd done. "The company jet will be prepped for a five a.m. takeoff. Exetor, you're dismissed." Tiny smile still in place, the heir nodded his black head at her, indicating he'd appreciated her maneuver, undercutting Rolex's move.

Now, if the younger Exetor didn't have another exit line... She waited, breath held, her back to Rolex.

Finally, she heard him stomping off and released the breath—only to realize he'd left her alone with the bigger, scarier shark.

"Um. Right-hand man. Why me?"

"Right-hand woman, Ms. Rothschild." His smile widened. "Because we proved in the alley we're a good team."

"The alley...?"

He leaned to one side—revealing a bust of his grandfather on the credenza behind him. She'd seen, but hadn't consciously realized, that it was now topped by a helmet.

A glossy black motorcycle helmet—with the identifying eagle and trident above its visor.

Recognition stunned her. "*You* rescued me."

"I disagree. You and I worked together to defeat those muggers. *We* rescued you and your pet."

"I didn't do anything."

"Besides a well-aimed kick? You protected Fido. That was your main job on our team."

"Fido?" She blinked, understanding coming a moment later. "He's not a dog. He's a cat."

Lovless grimaced. "I don't like cats. Still, you protected your pet, we worked together, and we accomplished the mission. And I appreciate your assist with Junior." He nodded his chin at the doorway where Rolex had recently tried to get in the last word.

Elizabeth's cheeks heated. She'd done it because Rolex had kicked her once too often, and she didn't want to see the newcomer get kicked, too.

But the powerful, leather-clad man from the alley didn't need her pitiful help. He could take care of himself. Very, *very* well.

"We leave at oh-dark-thirty." He turned his attention to a stack of papers. Pulled off the first, scanned it, snared Landy's fountain pen from his decorative set, and signed the paper with slashes of strong black ink. "You'd better go pack."

"Oh. Right." She rose. Hesitated. "What sorts of things do I need to pack?" Parachutes? Emergency rations? Her Girl Scout camp kit?

His silver-blue gaze rose, colliding with hers so hard she felt it like a physical hit. Her stomach lurched, and her breath sped up.

"It's an island paradise, but you'll be working hard. Then again, there's a five-star resort and your teammates are all rich men. Bring what you think is appropriate. I'm going with shorts, a suit, and a utility knife—and a shield for my back."

*　　*　　*

Elizabeth left Landy's office—*no, not Landy's*. She'd been wrong about nothing being changed. *Everything* had. Despite the pictures all being the same, despite not a stick of furniture being moved, that had definitely no longer been Landy's office.

The black motorcycle helmet had cemented it. The placement of it, on his grandfather's bust, visor covering the older face...whether intentional or not, that helmet marked the younger Lovless' territory.

Conflicted feelings rose in her breast. Landy had told her to beware the heir. His grandson rejected everything he stood for.

But Landy wasn't here. The heir was. To keep the charities intact, didn't she have to embrace the new, or even, as Preston said, try to tame him?

Any. Way. A shudder of both lust and shame went through her.

Though, her new boss might prove impossible to tame. Terror added to the mix. What would happen to Landy's charities then?

Against all that, she remembered the big biker rescuing her in the alley, her sheer relief—and her shiver of purely feminine response.

Emotions tangled inside her, but strangely, as she opened the door to her small office, they all resolved into one surge of feeling—hope.

Hope for *what,* though, she wasn't sure.

"There you are." Ainsley looked up from teasing a paper puff on a string at the yellow kitten. "Sugar Lumpkins and I were starting to worry."

The small cat pounced on the paper, grabbing it with tiny claws. He *whumped* onto his back with an ungainly roll to scrabble at the paper with his hind legs.

Elizabeth, in spite of her roiling feelings, smiled. "We're not calling him Sugar Lumpkins."

"You have a better name? How'd the big meeting go?" Ainsley dropped the string to knot her hair at the back of her head, securing it with a couple pencils. "You still have a job?"

"For now. I'm leaving in the morning for a retreat. Can I ask you and Harper," she named their third roommate, "to take care of..." She trailed off, watching the kitten bat and gnarl at the tangle of string, wondering what to call the small predator.

"Sugar Puss?" Ainsley supplied brightly.

"Not Sugar anything." Elizabeth opened the carrier, took the impromptu toy, and managed to lure the small cat into the tote. "Come on. The kitten needs food and litter. Maybe I'll think of a name by the time we get home."

"You can't keep calling him 'the kitten.' How about Honey Whiskers?"

"How about not. How about..." Elizabeth surprised herself by saying, "*Fido.*"

*   *   *

Reb sat behind the aircraft carrier of a desk—sitting still, something he very rarely did, preferring to be active and in the field. But in this case he had an excuse. He was stunned.

He replayed the sway of Elizabeth's hips as she swiveled from the office on those impossibly high heels. He was right that they'd been in her messenger bag—and definitely wrong about her being anything approaching ordinary.

She was gorgeous. He'd always disliked cool blondes, having learned from his rich-kid childhood that they were cold and aloof.

Elizabeth wasn't cold or aloof. She might have been cool, but that only made him want to touch her, to caress her creamy skin to see if he could warm it under his fingertips. To see if he could heat it to anything approaching his own broiling temperature.

Damn it. Why her, why now?

A week ago Monday, he'd been on a mission, in country with his team. Then he'd gotten the news that his grandfather was dead, and he'd had to return to deal with the old bastard's legacy—the conglomerate.

His brothers didn't need the money, and he didn't want it. Hell, he didn't want anything to do with the old man. Reb was utterly focused on washing his hands of the whole thing and getting back to his team. He'd scheduled the meeting to hand Lovless Industries off to the board. Sure, they'd strip it of its assets. More power to them. A robber baron's legacy, devoured by his cronies and their get. Seemed appropriate.

But IEDs and craptastic missions had taught him never to be rash. So, in the meantime and to be thorough, he'd gone over the paperwork.

The charities had surprised him.

The old man, in the last two years of his life, had grown a conscience. And that conscience had a name—Elizabeth Rothschild.

Reb didn't want the money, and his billionaire brothers didn't need it, but Elizabeth's charities *did*. The conglomerate, stripped of its assets, couldn't support these worthy causes—and the ghouls left on the board certainly wouldn't.

That was when he'd changed plans. Keep the conglomerate in the family, but build a better board to run it. Friday, he'd arranged the teambuilding exercise to get rid of dead weight and pummel what was left into shape. He tapped his middle brother to lead it.

Lucas Lovless could don the mask of rich, entitled snob with the best of them. Reb's brother owned—more like collected—a string of nightclubs, casinos, and cars. Both men and women loved him. He'd have the old wolves barking his tune in no time.

Then, today, Reb had walked into that boardroom and seen *her,* surrounded and harried by that pack of stupidly selfish wolves. Need rose hot and urgent inside him, demanding he protect her himself.

Another change of plans. Stay long enough to make her safe.

He downplayed his urgency by telling himself that he'd have helped any woman in danger. But Elizabeth… intrigued him.

She was a walking contradiction, plain, lumpy hat, but sleek, rich hair beneath. Soft-looking woman in a hard business. Running charities amid a bunch of money-grubbing rich. In personal danger in the alley, yet her first act was to protect her pet.

Despite everything, she was a fighter, in the alley and standing up to the board, men who'd obliterate her if they could.

That kind of courage had to be honored.

It had nothing to do with her sweet, soft eyes—not blue, not gray, not hazel nor brown, but some soothing, deep combination of them all—that Reb decided to cover the exercise himself. Not because of her eyes or because she turned his pelvis into a mass of aching, tight need.

Really?

He rolled his eyes at himself. In the final analysis, *why* didn't matter. He picked up the phone to call off his brother. Taking the teambuilding exercise himself meant putting off his return to his SEAL team, and that wrenched his gut.

But Elizabeth needed him.

Chapter Five

The plane touched down on a runway hewn from tropical jungle. Elizabeth's stomach refused to land with it. Too excited...nervous...flustered? She was looking forward to this but didn't know why.

An island teambuilding exercise? Like an extreme sports reality show with a country-club of suits. She shouldn't be excited; she should be appalled.

Following the line of linen-suited men down the boarding stairs, she stepped into a warm, soft breeze. The air caressed her cheeks and filled her nose with exotic scents she couldn't name but which were redolent of green, moist, growing things.

She'd worn her business heels and a business jacket, but underneath was a simple sundress. In a rare sense of abandon, as she stepped onto the tarmac, she removed the jacket, to enjoy the sun and breeze on her bare arms.

A line of stretch limousines waited for them. Draping the jacket over her rolling carryon, Elizabeth extended the handle and started for the last one.

A touch on her arm stopped her. "You're with me."

She turned to find Landon Lovless III towering over her.

"Mr. Lovles—"

"Good lord." He stared down at her. "What if you're trying to get my attention because a piano is falling toward my head? I'd be dead before you got that mouthful out."

For some reason, the image of a plummeting baby grand tickled her funny bone. "You have that many pianos falling on your head?" Normally, she didn't tease the sharks, and nothing before this had indicated he had a sense of humor, but the day was too fine and the words bubbled out.

But he rewarded her with a big grin that was almost boyish. "Not usually. With this group, though, I think it best to be prepared." He held out a hand, indicating the first limo. "Call me Reb."

Not a name she'd have expected. She rolled her carryon toward the sleek vehicle. "Why Reb?"

"Short for Rebel. A handle I got early in my Navy days."

"You're Navy?"

"SEAL. And I can't wait to get back to my team."

Strangely, that gave her a twinge of disappointment. *Why, when it'd be easier to install Preston in his place?*

At the limo, the driver took her carryon. "What about our bags?"

"They'll be waiting at the hotel."

Rolex was already inside the limo, hogging the bucket seat nearest the door, where he could "accidentally" trip anyone else trying to get in. Elizabeth's shoulders sagged. She was so tired of the relentless dominance games. Squaring her shoulders, she mentally stoked herself to climb over Rolex.

Lovless stopped her with a barring arm and bent to peer inside. "Move over, Junior."

"Don't call me Junior." The younger Exetor leaned out to scowl up at the heir.

Lovless—Reb—only smiled back, as if he'd been angling for pissing off Junior and had won. Seeing his advantage evaporate, Rolex's scowl deepened, but he slid over two seats.

Elizabeth's whole body lightened. She could fight the old boys, but it was nice not to have to. Nice to spend her energy enjoying the beautiful day.

Reb handed her in. As Elizabeth settled into the clean, comfortable, cream leather bucket, he grabbed the door frame and swung himself onto the seat recently vacated by Exetor then shut the door. The limo started out.

"Not Junior?" Reb said to Rolex. "What do you want me to call you?"

Rolex's nose went up. "*Mister* Exetor will do."

"All right," he said agreeably. "But don't blame me if I'm only halfway through, 'Mr. Exetor, look out,' and you get hit in the head with a piano."

"A piano?" The shark's scowl was momentarily blanked by a puzzled frown.

"Apparently, there's an epidemic of falling pianos here," Elizabeth supplied helpfully.

Reb rewarded her with that boyish grin, sparkling white and charming, so unlike anything she'd ever seen from the old men on the board.

"You think this is a joke?" Exetor Junior snarled.

"You want serious?" Reb leaned across her to nail Rolex with a low and deadly tone. "I've fallen on homemade bombs and hoped and prayed my Kevlar could take it, and

I've watched buddies get shot up by insurgents. *That* was serious. *This* isn't."

Elizabeth's breath caught in her chest. From playful to deadly serious in the blink of an eye. But if he had in fact lived with that kind of danger, this wasn't the spoiled, rebellious kid Landy had led her to believe.

Rolex stuttered, "Th-the conglomerate—"

"Money isn't everything, *Mr.* Exetor." Reb sat back. "I've learned to laugh while I can."

Silence reigned. By the tracking of Rolex's eyes, he was scrambling for a comeback. Finally, he leaned forward and sneered, "You're a military hardass, I get it. So what crude cabin do you have us crammed into?" He gave a theatric expression of horror. "Or are we staying in *tents?*"

"Neither," Reb replied. "I decided you were right. These men aren't used to deprivation or working together for the common good. One lesson at a time. You and the rest of the board are staying at the resort."

"Well, good. You've seen reason at last—"

"But you're working in the village."

"What?"

"That's the teambuilding exercise. One side of the island is paradise. The other, not so much. We'll be building a house for one of the desperately poor."

Elizabeth got a surge of pleasure at that—until she realized he didn't mean just funding the building. "With our own hands?"

"Don't be ridiculous." Rolex launched himself back into his seat with crossed arms. "That's an awful use of our time. Hire a contractor."

Shockingly, she almost agreed with him. She was middling good with a screwdriver, but a hammer, not so much, as her often-bruised thumbs and toes would attest. And power tools? She was the original reason they'd invented patching compound. Although it would be interesting to watch the old guard get their hands dirty.

"Where's the fun in that?" Reb looked smug as the limo pulled to a stop. "Here we are. Get your room, get squared away. The bus leaves in one hour."

He opened the door, revealing a tall, curved, modern hotel. As he slid out on his long legs, that green scent again invaded Elizabeth's nostrils, and the slapping of ocean waves echoed in her ears. A sense of peace settled inside her. Maybe it wouldn't be so bad.

Grabbing the door frame, Reb leaned back inside to glare at Exetor Junior. "One hour."

"Or else what?" Rolex challenged.

"Anyone not on that bus—is fired."

That smacked the smug off Junior's face. It also made Elizabeth jerk with surprise, her peace evaporating.

Reb offered his hand to her. Off-balance from his threat of firing, she took it. His fingers, closing around her hand, engulfed it. A shock of recognition shimmered deep inside her as he pulled her easily from her seat.

She tottered a moment on her heels, and he grasped her by the upper arms to steady her. His hands branded her with heat that shivered through her. At the contact, skin to skin, her gaze flew up to his, colliding with his rapidly dilating pupils ringed by silver irises.

Releasing her slowly, he let a tiny, knowing smile curl his lips. "You should probably change into your runners."

"If we're building a house, yes." Her voice emerged breathy, almost husky, from her throat. This close, she could smell him, the spicy tang of his masculinity. Feel his heat.

Her heart raced in her chest. If they'd been alone...

"Move it, Elizabeth," Rolex grumped from behind. "I only have an hour to prepare, or I'm fired, apparently. C'mon, get going."

Jumping away from the younger Exetor's ramming knees, she managed tartly, "Or *we're* fired. It's not all about you."

Reb wasn't her lover, he was her boss—and more, they weren't alone, and they'd never be alone, surrounded by sharks. She got going.

Chapter Six

Elizabeth, in shorts, a tank style T-shirt, ponytail, and runners—for those plummeting pianos—boarded the rickety old school bus. As she scanned down the aisle for a friendly face, it reminded her of braving the boardroom yesterday. Like yesterday, the faces scattered through the seats all scowled, whether topped by silver, dark, or no hair. But unlike the boardroom, these scowls contained a hint of discomfort. Concern. A few even looked anxious. *Welcome to my world, boys.*

Reb wasn't here yet, or maybe he'd gone ahead to the building site. She felt a ping of disappointment but convinced herself it was just the scowls.

She glanced to her right. The beaming round face of the driver, who sat behind the wheel clad in a casual uniform of khaki shorts and resort-logoed shirt, brought her spirits up. She gave him a grateful smile in return. Then with a sigh, she chose the least-threatening scowl, Preston Hare's, and started back.

As she passed rows of half-empty seats, she glanced down to see what the sharks were wearing. Cargo shorts.

Golf shirts or short-sleeve cotton or silk Oxfords. Almost as if the combination was a uniform.

And sandals with dark socks.

Not only a fashion nightmare, but what if someone dropped a hammer on their toes?

Or one of those ubiquitous pianos.

She couldn't help herself—the visual lightened her whole mood.

"What are *you* smiling for?" Preston grumped. "There's absolutely nothing to be happy about. This is a disaster."

"A runaway disaster," she agreed, sliding in beside him. "So, why not enjoy what we can?"

"You're not making sense." Her ex turned his glare out the window.

"I guess not." Her smile widened.

"Lovless was supposed to resign. *I* was supposed to be chairman of the board by now. A disaster."

"If it helps, I think Reb doesn't want to be running the board any more than we want him."

"*Reb?*" Preston's gaze shot back to her, his head twisting from the window with an almost comic snap.

"He told me to call him that." An imp rose up, making her add, "Because of the pianos."

"I have no idea what that means. But if you're making romantic progress, we can use that." He gave her a raptor's smile that made her feel slightly sick.

Just then, the bus started off with a jerk and a belch of black smoke. Elizabeth grabbed the seat in front of her to keep from being thrown to the floor. As the engine ground up through the gears, talking became impossible. She was grateful. Preston's gaze spoke loud enough for him. Glittering, rapacious, encouraging her to pull out all the stops to get the Lovless heir in bed and pliable.

Yuck.

Sure, she wanted to have power on the board. Needed it, to keep her promise to Landy. To make a real difference in the world.

As she jounced on her seat, she gazed at Preston. He was supposed to be her champion with Landy gone. *That* wasn't happening.

Which left Reb. Sex should have been an obvious weapon in her arsenal. But luring him with her body or trapping him emotionally didn't seem fair or right.

Not that thoughts of Reb didn't bring thoughts of sex. That tall, dark, powerful form was made for bedding. But not sex as a weapon.

Sex as a meeting of bodies. A sharing of attraction. A deepening of real emotions...

For as long as it took him to leave.

Heaving a disgusted sigh, she turned her attention to the window beyond Preston. Acres of pristine white sand awed her, and water so blue it hurt her eyes. The heavy, humid scent of vegetation and flowers was muted by the tang of bus exhaust, but not completely covered. Nothing could put down such exuberance.

That was how she felt around Reb. All her life, she'd been about duty and accomplishment. Reb made her feel simply alive.

The buildings went from luxurious, widely spaced, multi-story structures in clean, white stucco and cream brick to shoulder-to-shoulder single-story, rickety frame buildings. Just as clean, and brightly painted in all the hues of the rainbow.

"Garish," Preston sneered.

"Simply alive," Elizabeth murmured.

The bus soon stopped.

"About time," her ex grumbled, rising.

Elizabeth stood and eased into the line of board members cuing up for the door to open. She bent to peer out while she waited. The street looked residential. Low, one-story houses sat on shallow lots, the homes' small windows shuttered against the rising heat of the day. Slightly slanted roofs made the dwellings look like Lego heads with ball caps. No sidewalks, no curbs, and no grass, but no weeds either. A few trees clung to open ground. A tidy neighborhood park sat in the next block.

Outside her window was a house frame of clean bright wood, several workers putting up Tyvek wrap, others placing plywood on the roof. Elizabeth released a sigh of relief. She thought they might have to start from the ground up. But it looked like they'd have help, and experienced help at that.

The bus door hissed open. As board members trooped off, Elizabeth was struck by the difference in physiques, not usually so apparent under tailored suits. Stringy hatchet-men, the old men tubby or flabby, and even the younger men were more like wire and wet clay, especially compared to the construction workers, tanned and healthy with broad shoulders and, from the few who worked with their shirts off, well-muscled. One man on the roof was well and truly ripped.

She came off the bus and stood a moment, hanging onto the door, staring at him. Placing plywood and nailing it in place with an old-fashioned hammer, the man was a symphony of strength in motion. Mounds of muscle bunched and eased, sliding hypnotically under smooth, oiled, tanned skin. Heat pooled in her hips, watching him. She took a couple involuntary steps closer, wanting to see more. To touch that sun-brushed skin, to kiss and lick and maybe nibble...

The man turned to the newcomers and waved. Reb.

Elizabeth screeched to a halt, suddenly flustered. She'd been inches from panting. Touching her cheek, she found it hot with embarrassment.

He dropped lightly off the roof and strode toward an older man standing with a binder under his arm, his dark face beginning to sheen in the heat. From the way the man's keen, dark eyes surveyed the work, and the silver touching his tightly curled hair, Elizabeth thought he might be in charge of the site.

As Reb neared, she realized his skin wasn't completely smooth. Several thin scars showed silver against the bronze—including a thicker, wickedly ragged line across one round, powerful biceps.

Grabbing a towel from a small table near the foreman, Reb wiped the back of his neck and his torso, making his chest muscles jump appealingly. Elizabeth swallowed hard. He tossed the cloth to one side and snatched a second piece, which turned out to be a skin-tight shirt when he winched it over his arms with a flare of lats. Her swallow stuck in her throat. By dint of repeated effort, she managed to get her swallow down by the time he rolled the tee along his torso and into place.

Dressed, Reb wrapped an arm around the older man's shoulders and brought him to where the group milled.

"This is Bob Leconte. He's our general contractor and the guy who's going to make sure our building is up to code—despite you tadpoles."

Exetor Senior rolled his eyes. "We have questions, we ask Bob, we get it."

"No, you *don't* get it. Bob doesn't have time for noob questions. He has a team of experts to supervise—who in turn will supervise you. You ask *them* your questions."

"Middle management," Preston muttered.

"Bob and I have teams set up." Slicing Preston a dirty glare, Reb began calling out names. "Roland Exetor Senior, Preston Hare, Charles Harvey. You're on painting duty with Sam." He pointed to a tall, thin man standing beside a set of cans.

"Painting?" Exetor Senior objected. "I'm wearing a designer silk shirt. What if I get paint on it?"

Reb only snorted a laugh. "You want to hang drywall instead? That's over fifty pounds a sheet."

"I can lift fifty pounds."

"Yes, but can you lift it past waist level and hold it one handed while you fumble around with drywall screws?"

"There are machines to do that."

"Not here, there aren't. Tomorrow, wear something you don't mind getting messy. Drywall team." He called off more names. "You're over there. Dust masks and safety glasses are beside the sheetrock. Your supervisor is..."

He went on, and Elizabeth waited, trying to be patient, for her duties. But honestly, she was getting excited. She'd spent her life trying to make a difference. Building an actual home? That was making a difference on a most fundamental scale. A direct impact on a person's life.

So, she was almost disappointed when Reb called, "Rothschild, Exetor Junior, you're with me."

"I can help with building," she said as she trotted up. "You don't have to make me the go-fer just because I'm female."

A smile played on his lips. "I'm not. You're not. Nobody drives but the locals. Traffic takes a bit of getting used to, here."

"Then what are we doing, Lovless?" Rolex asked.

"This whole exercise is about teamwork. The board has to get used to following orders when I call the play. But in a good team, information runs both ways—orders go down the chain, listening comes up. You're my ears. Go around to each of the teams. Join in, do the work alongside them, and really listen. Then meet me for lunch. We'll go over what you've learned then."

With a roll of eyes exactly like his father's, Exetor Junior stalked off.

But before Elizabeth could leave, Reb turned on her, fists on hips and gaze narrow. "And in the cause of information flow—exactly *what* were you staring at when you first arrived?"

Chapter Seven

Staring at? More like drooling over Reb's tanned, muscular torso. Elizabeth touched her breastbone. "Um...you?"

His eyes narrowed, that knife-like silver that seemed like a scalpel to her thoughts.

Make this professional, quick. "I mean, look at you. You can handle this all yourself. You don't need Junior and me. You're a SEAL, best of the best, not afraid of anything." She pointed at the long scar on his biceps, the tail running under his sleeve. "A bunch of cranky rich men can't possibly compare to falling on an IED."

His gaze relaxed, and he shook his head. "That scar's from a disagreement with a crocodile. The IED didn't make a mark. But you're wrong. I get afraid."

"You do?"

"Sure. I was scared off my ass with that IED. I was too busy fighting the croc to worry." He gave her a wry smile. "But the bomb...I remember laying there, milliseconds ticking away that felt like hours. I knew I'd *probably* be okay, but probably isn't for sure. If *anything* went wrong—my placement on the device, my vest, anything—I'd be losing body parts. Worse, turning myself into more shrapnel." His blue eyes clouded with memory. "Hurting my team instead of protecting them. Yeah, those moments were like years, and scary."

His pain was deeply personal. She was touched he'd chosen to share it with her. "You knew all that, but you still jumped on the explosive?"

"I had to." His gaze met hers, clearing. "Lives were on the line. And I do trust my gear. My gear, my training, and my team have gotten me through seemingly impossible missions. But..."

She followed his gaze to where Roland Exetor Junior stood apart from a couple hatchet men, watching them awkwardly chuck construction debris into a dumpster rather than joining in with the work. His disgusted expression said exactly what he thought of the manual labor.

Turning back, she saw emotions crossing Reb's features in quick succession. Anger, impatience, resignation, amusement. He sighed. "But we're all human."

Elizabeth's heart lurched. His face, in that unguarded moment, was even more expressive than Rolex's.

"We're all driven by personal goals and inner demons." Reb tipped his head at Junior as his gaze came back to hers.

"Not everyone is immature and self-serving," she said without thinking. Except, she'd believed that of Reb before actually meeting him. Her veins filled with shame.

"Maybe, but even when our intentions are pure, we make mistakes. We try hard, but we're human, you know? So yeah, maybe I could handle this all by myself—if it weren't for bad luck and bad timing. Misfires happen. That's why I need you and Junior."

She began to understand. "You want us to listen to the teams to catch the problems board members can't, or *won't*, share. So the mission gets done with them—or in spite of them."

He blinked at her as if surprised by her response. His lips parted, but instead of speaking, he only continued to stare at her. Finally he managed, "I'm pleased you understand. But who's Rolex...? Oh, Roland Exetor. *Rolex.*" He laughed, boyish and carefree.

The laugh, his pleasure and lightheartedness, tickled her with delight. It was appealing, even more so for the pain in his eyes only a moment before.

Understanding better what he needed from her and why, she went to join her first team.

*　　*　　*

After Elizabeth left, Reb strode inside the developing house to watch the board members work. Do his own reconnaissance.

But his gaze kept finding her.

She painted beside Exetor Senior, his soiled silk fussy beside her simple shorts and tank. The cool blonde was sexy in skirt and heels, but when she was working, wisps of hair escaped her ponytail, her skin shone with exertion, and her whole body glowed with health.

Beyond sexy. Just ask his hardening groin.

Eventually, she laid down her brush and moved off to join another group. He followed her with his gaze, enjoying the sway of her hips.

She'd surprised him. Other women had asked about his scar and the IED. He'd recounted that incident lots of times—though it was strange he'd admitted fear to her so soon after meeting her. For some reason, he wanted to be completely straight with her. He'd only admitted to one or two people that he'd been scared.

She'd been amazingly admiring and sympathetic, but that wasn't what surprised him.

His feet automatically took him in the direction she'd gone and found she'd joined the trim and molding detail. Job scheduling was a mess, every area of the house in a different phase of completion. But with the largely volunteer workforce, it was the only way to get multiple jobs with different skill levels available at once.

She bent to get a piece of baseboard, showing him a nice line of calf, thigh, and shapely hip.

Groin tightening, he swallowed hard and turned away. She'd been admiring and sympathetic, but he'd gotten sympathy and admiration before. Truth be told, he'd seen plenty of nice, shapely lines before, too.

But Elizabeth...she'd understood, not just the story, but what *he'd* learned from it. Despite never having been military, she'd not only understood, but took the lesson to her own heart. The mission was paramount. Trust your team and equipment, but not only did no plan survive meeting the enemy, sometimes your own people made mistakes and bad choices. Information received, understood, and adopted. He'd never told her directly, but she understood her job was to find out what was going on in the trenches so he could adjust the mission for it anyway.

That was what surprised him about Elizabeth. Her whole-hearted help. She wasn't just on a mission. She was on *his* mission.

His teammate.

His heart squeezed hard once before resettling into its steady, reliable rhythm.

He'd been furious his grandfather had saddled him with Lovless Industries. He'd spent his whole adult life making himself the opposite of the greedy robber baron. Ever since he'd flown back to New York, he had one goal. Get out of here and get back to his real team, the SEAL operators who understood him. The *only* people who understood him.

Now Elizabeth seemed to understand him, too.

He didn't know what to think of that.

Well, only one solution. Do recon.

This time, his information-gathering would be on Elizabeth Rothschild herself.

*   *   *

"Get me another board, Elizabeth." Preston Hare pointed at a long piece of trim.

As she stooped to pick up the baseboard molding, sweat trickled into her eyes. This was her third detail in as many hours. Between the rising heat of the day and her own exertion, she'd gone from perspiring to full-blown sweat. But she had a job to do, and she wasn't going to let a little thing like physical discomfort stand in her way.

Straightening, she wiped her forehead with the back of one hand before handing the board to Preston. He got to play with power tools while she'd been relegated to fetching, normally not something she'd do. She tried not to let any man use her.

But, mindful of Reb's desire to mold the LI board into a team, she was trying to foster an environment of teamwork by cooperating.

She wasn't sure it was working.

Her ex placed the trim against the floor crookedly and prepared to hammer it home with the nail gun.

"Wait." One of the professionals stopped him. "First, we need to see if this is level." He put a long tool on top of the board. A bubble floated to the center. "Looks good. Now, find the studs. See where the drywall screws are?" He slid a pencil from his shirt pocket and notched marks on the wall near the floor. "That's where you want to attach the trim."

"Great. Move." Preston brandished the nail gun.

"Patience." The supervisor pointed at the bottom of the trim. "See the gaps?"

"Who cares? The carpet will cover it."

"Let's just listen to the professional, okay?" Elizabeth put her hand on his wrist. Preston rolled his eyes but lowered the gun. "What do we do?"

"Push the board tight against the wall." the man replied as he fit his pencil in a compass.

She pressed one side tight and glared at Preston. After a moment, he held the other end.

The professional opened the compass the height of the widest gap. Keeping the needle on the floor, he drew the contraption along the board. The pencil made a slightly wavy line. "This scribes the trim to the contour of the floor."

"That's cool." She watched him work, his movements precise, sure. "Now what?"

"Now, I cut away the excess. I'll be right back."

He took the board away. Elizabeth stood and turned to her ex. "How's the work going so far?"

"Guess." His mouth twisted. "I don't know what Lovless thinks he's proving with this."

"Teamwork? Building something that matters?"

"How is this better than hiring a crew? What have you been doing, anyway?"

The board members wouldn't talk freely if they knew her real job, so she only said, "I painted. Steadied a few pieces of drywall." Working alongside them, hoping they'd gossip and she could listen in.

All she'd gotten for her trouble was hot, dusty, and liberally spattered with paint.

Preston *tsked.* "That's all? You're sweating like a pig. Tired from just a little brushing and lift-and-carry? How are you going to prove you deserve to run with the big dogs? You need to do better."

Her shoulders hunched at his hit. "I can't help it if the tools and materials are sized for big guys with shoulders and muscles and—"

"Elizabeth." He took her by the arms. "You need to be a helluva lot tougher to be Lovless' right-hand man."

"Right-hand *woman.*"

"*Whatever.* Lovless is military. That's good news, because it means he'll be going back to whatever hellhole he came from. But it's bad news for you, because he'll only respect stamina and strength."

"Here we go." The construction professional returned with the trim. "Now, let's snug this up tight, and you can put those nails in where the pencil marks are. One in the base, one in the stud."

As she knelt to help hold the board, a strand of hair escaped from her ponytail, sticking to her eyes and cheek. One handed, she shoved the hair away, wishing she could shove away the real annoyance.

Was her ex right? Did she need to work, not only alongside the men, but *outwork* them?

Reb said her job on the team was to filter into various groups and listen. But Preston was usually pretty savvy.

Maybe Reb wanted her to do both, listen for problems, but also show she could work every bit as hard as the men.

Reb doesn't care.

Maybe not. But Reb was leaving. She needed to show Exetor Senior and the others she was tough enough to stay.

Prove her place on the board.

Besides, so far, she hadn't gotten a whole lot of information. Maybe if she proved she could work as hard as any of them, she could gain their trust—and with their trust, get them to spill their problems.

Despite the heat of the day, she poured on the energy.

*   *   *

Just before lunch, Reb was cleaning off his putty knife when silver-domed Roland Exetor Senior sidled up to him. His back automatically went up. Then he remembered Elizabeth's nickname for Exetor's son. Rolex. That tickled him, easing his anger. It let him see Exetor Senior not as his grandfather's robber-baron crony, but as an old man, tired from honest work.

The paint splatter on Senior's fancy silk shirt was a sure sign he'd had too much on the brush. His painting supervisor would've told him how to dip the bristles and scrape off the excess, but the old man hadn't listened. Either he'd learn to listen, or he'd be buying a lot of shirts.

That amused him as well.

Before Senior could start in on bitching, Reb slid in, "So, how much did your painting supervisor have to redo?"

"Supervisor." The elder's tone was scornful. "I could buy and sell a hundred of that man."

"Aside from the fact that human trafficking is illegal and immoral, I think the person who moves into this house would prefer 'that man' sells a hundred of *you.*"

The old man's jaw dropped. Speechless, for a moment.

Reb simply smiled. Building a house, meeting Elizabeth for lunch, annoying Exetor Senior...this day was going quite well.

Then a crafty glint entered Exetor's eye. "You know, son, I didn't think you had it in you."

Reb had been in too many mortally dangerous situations not to recognize one now. "I'm not your son."

"No. But you remind me of my Roland. Your grandfather would be proud of you."

Gritting his teeth, he forced himself not to respond to the obvious trap. Though he was sure his face must've said what he was thinking. *What the hell do you mean?*

Exetor, the old wolf, replied just as if Reb spoke the words. "Leveraging your power with the board to force us here. Coercing us into menial labor. Well done."

The false heartiness in the other man's tone made him sick.

Eyes glinting maliciously, he delivered the final gut punch. *"You're just like your old man."*

Reb flinched as if he'd been actually hit.

Exetor saw. With a final grin, he stalked away, leaving Reb bleeding, stunned, angry—and for the first time, unsure.

He'd run away from home and joined the Navy not just to get away from the abomination his grandfather was—he'd gotten out the moment he realized he was being molded into a duplicate copy.

But if Exetor was to be believed, somehow, from beyond the grave, the old man had done exactly that anyway.

Chapter Eight

The idea of becoming his scoundrel of a grandfather made Reb want to fall on the IED again, this time without the vest.

Then Elizabeth came out of the house to grab a moment's breeze. Her paint-spattered tank clung to her damp body, outlining every gorgeous curve, revealing the perk of her nipples.

He stood there, stunned in a different way. In heels and makeup, the cool blonde was lovely. Bedraggled, wet like she'd been in a sauna, she'd never looked so beautiful to him.

Bedraggled. Wet like a sauna. He looked closer. Her hair straggled from its ponytail, tendrils lying limp alongside her face. She wasn't glowing with exertion now. She was dripping, exhausted. Her smudged shorts hung low on her hips, as if she'd lost weight in just the last four hours.

Anger fired through him on her behalf. Damn it, she was working herself too hard.

Time to put to use some of that autocratic command he'd apparently inherited from his grandfather.

But, unlike the old man, Reb would use it to help someone other than himself.

*　　*　　*

Elizabeth felt Reb's blazing anger warping the air before she turned and actually saw him stalking up to her, flames in his eyes.

She was too tired to care. So, when he seized her by the arm and walked her away from the house, she let him. In truth, his supporting strength was rather nice.

Then he bent to her ear. "Damn it, Elizabeth. You were only supposed to do enough work to listen in." His voice was low, meant for her ears only. "You've run yourself ragged."

Answering anger fired her own veins, poking through her lethargy. "They weren't talking," she hissed back. "I had to prove myself to them."

"Lunch?" Rolex called, trotting up behind them. "Please say we're not eating out of a bag like a horse."

Rows of paper bags stood on a nearby table. A sweating tapper cooler, filled with pale yellow liquid wafting the tang of lemon, sat beside the bags, along with a stack of paper cups.

"We *were*." Reb's tone was exasperated. "But I think we need to get Elizabeth into some air conditioning."

And she'd been afraid he would fault her for not giving everything she had to gather information? He was treating her like a damsel in distress.

"I'm not feeble," she snarled.

"I'm not risking you keeling over," he snarled back.

That was too much. She yanked her arm from his grip, but overdid the action, stumbled, and nearly fell.

Reb's strong arm lassoed her, cinching her into a torso hard as concrete. "Damn, you're stubborn." As she wriggled to get away, he softened it with a small smile, meant only for her. "I've always had a soft spot for stubborn. Stop wiggling, Rothschild. I get that you don't want to look weak. Don't worry. To the rest of the world, we look like two buddies out for a walk and talk."

Elizabeth's anger melted at that. *He understands.*

Her exhaustion, without anger to counter it, threatened to consume her. She leaned gratefully into him as they strolled toward an old pickup truck. He was amazing, really. They'd known each other less than two days. Yet he'd seen her plight and took steps to help. He already knew her well enough to read her without words?

Her belly flooded with hot desire, charged with the knowledge that here was a man who could see her most intimate desires.

Satisfy them.

And then leave her.

Damn it, Reb, why now?

Why had Preston Hare never shown her this kind of understanding and support? He'd been her boyfriend, for heaven's sake. *He* should have known her well enough.

Why this man she'd just met, this almost-stranger? Why was it *Reb* who made her feel warm and protected? Understood?

I have friends for that, she argued with herself. Ainsley and Harper were her emotional support. Which reminded her, she needed to text them, to let them know she'd gotten here okay.

But as she leaned heavily against Reb's strength, she realized he gave her physical support, too. The hard torso pressed, almost imprinted, against her side was strong, solid. The kind you could rely on. Pressed intimately to her own wet body...

Wasn't he disgusted by her perspiration wicking into his T-shirt? She tried to pull away.

"Hey," he said softly, tugging her more firmly into his side. "What are you doing?"

"I'm all sweaty."

"Nothing wrong with a bit of honest sweat. Means you were working hard. But now we're going to take a break."

At the truck, he opened the passenger door for her and handed her up onto a bench seat, leaving the door open for Rolex to slide in behind her. She scooted over into the middle—and nearly into Reb swinging into the driver's seat.

"I thought only locals could drive," Rolex said dryly as he got in.

"I've been here before. I learned the customs. Shut the door, belt yourself in, and hold on." He started the truck with a throaty *vroom*, and they took off.

Five harrowing minutes later, he pulled up in front of a diner with a faded wood sign proclaiming "FOOD."

"Classy," Rolex remarked.

Reb slanted a smile at them. "It's nearby, it's cool, and the FOOD is good."

Somehow Elizabeth heard the capital letters, and it tickled her funny bone.

The diner was indeed cool. Several locals were inside taking lunch breaks, but the moment Reb entered, a big woman bustled over and grabbed him in a hug.

"Rebel Lovless! Papa and I were hoping to see you. Come, sit. I have a table for you and your friends."

"This is Mama," he explained as the woman led them to a round table near the window. He pointed at a small, wiry man with a grease-stained apron waving from the kitchen. "She and Papa own the place."

"Thanks to you." She flapped her hands at two young men attired in mechanics' stained overalls already at the table. "Shoo. Reb is here."

"You got it, Mama." Still chewing, the young workers simply lifted their plates and moved to one of the long slab tables in the middle.

Elizabeth felt bad at having ousted them from their seats. "We don't want to inconvenience anyone."

"Those are my sons." Mama unleashed a dazzling white smile at her. "The fact they have any seats at all is because of this man. Won't hurt them to eat with the others. Sit, sit."

She bustled off, leaving Reb to pull out Elizabeth's chair.

She took her seat and glanced, curious, at him. "Mama seems to think you can walk on water. What did you do for her?"

"Nothing much." Color flagged his cheekbones as he settled onto the chair beside her. "I helped build this place."

Rolex took the third seat. "There aren't any menus."

His tone wasn't as scathing as she might have expected. Maybe hunger had blunted his attitude.

"We eat family style here. Mama brings out bowls of whatever is today's special, and we help ourselves."

"Sounds yummy." Exetor Junior might have been trying for a dry tone but he actually sounded interested.

Elizabeth, still curious, dared to poke a finger into Reb's biceps. Like poking a rock. "That isn't the whole story. How did you help?"

"See? Stubborn." He smiled. "Shore leave coincided with a volunteer project. I signed up as part of the work crew here."

"Unpaid?" Rolex's eyes widened comically. "You did *unpaid* labor on your vacation?"

"Not so different from your reading to sick kids at the hospital," Reb shot back.

Probably court-ordered community service, Elizabeth thought.

Until the other man's mouth snapped shut, his face red.

Surprise splashed her. That flustered blush said Rolex's reading was actual altruism. She hadn't known he had a kind bone in his body.

For the first time she felt a surge of optimism, that Reb's seed of charitable service might find a bit of fertile soil after all. She turned to him and said, "So, you hclpcd build the place, literally. But why does Mama treat you like a savior?"

"Oh, that. Well, I sort of took a bullet for Papa. Not a literal bullet," he hastened to add. "A load of shingles fell off the roof. They would have hit him."

Elizabeth pictured the small, wiry man struck by heavy shingles. "They'd have flattened him."

"Maybe, maybe not. He's sturdy like a mule. Still, I pushed him out of the way and caught the brunt of the load with my shoulder. I've trained in Judo, so I was able to roll most of the impact off."

"You save a man from grievous harm, then you roll off your own injury?" She blinked at him with eyes she was sure were as round as plates. "You know that's pretty impressive, right?"

His gaze came to her and something lit in it. His shoulders squared almost imperceptibly, and the smile he gave her promised he could be even more impressive, if she gave him a chance.

Then Rolex drawled, "A real hero," and the moment was broken.

A girl of about ten came out with a stack of plates and plastic cups followed by a boy of about six carrying napkin-wrapped utensils. Mama shepherded them both to the table. She carried a pair of big serving bowls.

"These are my oldest boy's kids." She introduced the two children as they laid the table. Then she herded them away again, leaving behind the bowls, which smelled of meat and potatoes and spices.

Rolex grabbed a spoon and served himself. Gravy dripped as he shoveled several healthy scoops onto his plate. He didn't make a single snide remark about the chipped bowls or peasant style food.

He must really be hungry. So was she.

Reb took the tongs from the second bowl and offered them to her. She used them to pinch up lacy lettuce, spinach, and shrimp coated with a glossy purple-red dressing. Sampling a bit, she tasted the best raspberry vinaigrette she'd ever had. "This is *good.*"

He smiled. "Don't let the homey looks mislead you. Mama and Papa studied at some of the best culinary schools there are. They actually met during a semester in France." He managed to get the spoon from Rolex and began to serve himself. "Now, what did you each find out?"

As they ate, Elizabeth admitted she hadn't heard anything that might be a problem.

"Was everyone working, though?" Reb asked.

"Yes. Not fast, mind you. Or terribly cleanly." She plucked at her paint-spattered tank shirt. "But they were all on their assigned projects, and doing a decent job."

"What about you, Exetor? Any issues?"

"Well, nobody's happy, as you might expect. Especially my father and his friends."

Elizabeth mentally substituted "old guard."

Rolex hesitated, then added, "There was one issue. I caught a pair of younger board members planning a small bit of sabotage."

Surprise stopped her fork midair. The idea that adult men would sabotage a charitable work simply to cause trouble for Reb was distressing. But why would Rolex actually reveal the information? Pointing out potential problems could only help the heir to the Lovless empire. She'd thought Rolex was solidly in the shark camp.

"Names?" Reb growled.

Rolex shook his head. "It wasn't that serious, and I took care of it. At this point, if I told you names, it would be more like tattling. What they planned was prank-level stuff, more embarrassing than damaging or injurious—or I would've said something before lunch."

"Why did you mention it at all?" Elizabeth asked.

"I don't think those two will try anything else, but where there's smoke...they're the first, but they won't be the last."

"And next time, it might be something less innocent." Reb forked up salad. "Got it. Frankly, I'm surprised it was younger board members. I'd have expected the hatchet men to act up first."

Elizabeth paused nibbling a shrimp. Reb thought of the hard-faced fixers on the board as hatchet men, too. She smiled slightly and wondered if he'd then know what she was talking about if she mentioned the old guard and young bucks.

"Fixers gotta fix." Rolex managed a grin around his spoon, though it looked slightly pained. "It doesn't mean they're not planning something. Only that they're more experienced hiding it."

True. Elizabeth pinched the bridge of her nose.

After lunch, Mama waved off Reb's money. He put away his wallet with a smile. "Another stubborn one," he noted to Elizabeth.

"Why aren't you making her take the money?" Rolex scraped the last gravy from his plate, licked the spoon clean then tossed it onto the plate and sat back with a sigh. "It's obvious they could use it."

"I respect pride. If they truly need something, they have only to ask. They know we're friends."

A warmth spread through her at that and held as Reb drove them back to the work site, where the paper lunch bags were gone and the lemonade was severely depleted.

As Rolex marched back to work, Reb caught her arm. "Elizabeth, wait."

Anger sparked in her blood. If he was going to caution her not to tire herself out or not bark with the big dogs or work too hard "honey," or anything vaguely sexist... She turned to him with a glare.

"You and I didn't get to talk much with Rolex there. How about I take you to dinner?"

Her simmering anger died in her confusion. "Dinner?"

"The resort has a couple five-star restaurants. It'll be a beautiful evening, and there's outdoor seating. Say yes?"

She felt her eyes widen. Dinner in a gorgeous alfresco setting on a romantic island? With most men it would be the first step in the dance of courtship.

Most men who aren't on the Lovless Industries board of directors, that is. They were a different breed, sharks whose one goal was making themselves a bigger profit. Romance was only another tool in their arsenal.

Logically, the heir to Lovless Industries was the biggest shark of them all.

But Reb was different, wasn't he?

She narrowed her gaze as if she could cut his intentions from his brain. "Is this business or pleasure?"

To her surprise, he searched her eyes before answering, and when he spoke, his tone was wistful. "What do you want it to be?"

Doubt ate at her. "Business." *I think.*

"Okay. Business it is." He released her arm.

She didn't know if she was pleased or not.

Chapter Nine

All afternoon, Elizabeth stewed on Reb's invitation to dinner.

Business or pleasure?

"What do you want it to be?"

Business, obviously. She didn't have time for pleasure, not with the board's sharks circling.

Yet something deep inside her ached for more.

Business.

Pleasure.

She still hadn't decided by the time she boarded the bus back to the hotel. Stumbling down the aisle, she saw no scowling faces this time. Only tired, sweaty men. She slumped onto an empty bench.

Preston Hare boarded a few minutes later and threw himself onto the seat beside her. "I saw you went off with Exetor and the heir at lunch." His gaze was a little too bright. "Did you seduce him yet?"

She briefly clenched her eyes. "No, we just had lunch."

"Well, hurry up, Elizabeth. We're here only a handful of days. He's obviously used to the best—you'll have your work cut out for you. You'd better get started."

Eww. What had she ever seen in Preston?

When the bus stopped at the resort hotel, she couldn't run away from her ex fast enough. Her room on the fourth floor was standard, but after working hard in the heat all day, it felt like paradise. The moment she was through the door, she stripped off her clothes, leaving a trail of humid lumps on her way to the shower.

Letting the hot water stream away the worst of her fatigue, she lectured herself on the many reasons this dinner *had* to be business only—while she shaved all her date areas. Treating herself to a romantic dinner would only backfire in the boardroom...but after toweling off, she slid silky scented lotion along her legs and stomach, spritzed herself with her good perfume, and retrieved her matching ice-blue lace bra and panties from the bureau.

Fine, she wanted to feel good underneath. As long as she kept her outside professional, everything would work out.

After a quick call to Ainsley to check on how she and Harper were getting along with kitten Fido—everyone was well—Elizabeth dressed.

She put up her hair in a sleek, no-nonsense chignon, then reached into the tiny hotel room closet for one of her severely tailored power suits.

Her hand fell on the one little black dress she'd brought.

Oh, who cares? Dinner in a romantic setting with a handsome man...

She plucked the dress from the hanger.

*   *   *

He'd made reservations on the terrace. Reb stood at the table as the host escorted her to a setting as romantic as the little-black-dress side of her could have hoped.

A white beach sparkled in the background, a cerulean blue sea glittering with emerald and ruby as it enfolded the setting sun. A gentle, warm breeze carried the aroma of sweet exotic flowers.

His eyes lit up seeing her. At that, her stomach sparkled like the beach. When he seated her, slipping the chair in with exquisite timing with her body, she couldn't help thinking they'd sync physically at other levels, too.

Taking the chair across from her, he slid the center candle to one side and reached for her hands. Not for a businesslike shake, but a full-on hand holding.

Now was the time to clarify that, despite her dress, she meant business.

But her whole body lit up at the contact, and frankly, she didn't want just business. She'd been business all day. Now, she wanted a little romance. Was that so wrong?

So, when he took her hands in his, she didn't stop him. When he stared deeply, soulfully into her eyes, his own burnished by the ocean background to a celestial blue, her whole being lifted, and she leaned toward him.

He opened his chiseled lips—to ask a question, she could see it in his gaze.

A *yes* bubbled up inside her, answer to any question he might ask.

"What did you think of Exetor's info, that those two young bucks were plotting trouble?"

She sighed. *Business then.* She shrugged, using the motion to slip her fingers from his grasp. "Convenient that Rolex didn't give us their names. But he didn't have to bring it up at all. Why lie?"

"To prove he was doing his job."

"And plant a seed of doubt or anger, I get it. But that's not Rolex's style." She waved her hand. "Oh, don't get me wrong. He's out for himself. But he's too arrogant to believe he has to stoop to lies and badmouthing others to get his way."

"What if he's trying to do the right thing?" Reb suggested with a strange hesitation. "Maybe he's honorable, in his own way, but he's been hemmed in by his father's expectations."

"Are we talking about the same man?" She frowned. Was Reb projecting his own situation on Rolex?

"Ah. Well, you know the players better than I do." He crooked a finger at the wine steward and, when the man joined them, ordered a bottle of what she recognized as a very fine *Sauvignon Blanc.*

Maybe tonight wasn't entirely about business. Her spirits rose. She shushed them. Probably, he just liked excellent wine.

Strange, though. Landy's heir might be expected to know good wine, but she wouldn't suppose it of the leather-clad motorcycle rider, the man who ate at cheap diners. Despite the rift between Reb and his grandfather being deep, maybe it wasn't complete.

As the wine steward left, a server swept up and dealt out plates of watered crackers and spinach-artichoke hummus. In his wake, the waiter appeared to recite a list of delicious options from memory. She ordered curry lentil soup with turmeric, quinoa, and edamame salad, and Moroccan chicken tagine with olives and salted lemons.

Reb ordered steak, rare.

She watched him chat with the waiter. The man was an enigma. In some ways, he seemed so unlike the sharks. Free of greed and avarice, down-to-earth, anti-everything the rest of the board stood for. The Rebel he was named.

But sometimes, he was so obviously Landy's grandson, commanding and autocratic and used to the very best, coming from so much money he could've swum through it like a certain duck.

The clothes he wore tonight certainly were more Lovless than Rebel. He cut a handsome line in his bespoke suit, Savile Row unless she missed her guess.

The wine steward returned with a bottle. He and Reb did a complex dance of cork, pour, swirl, and sip. At her companion's nod, the steward poured her glass full and topped off Reb's.

She tried her own swirl. The rivulets were thicker than she expected, good viscosity, and the motion opened a fine scent, sharp with lemon oil. She sipped. The taste, dry but fruity with an aftershock of nut creme, was excellent.

As the wine steward left, she remarked, "That's a nice suit."

Reb's cheeks darkened in that way she'd seen before. None of the other board members blushed as easily as he did. She found it rather endearing.

"I hope you don't take this the wrong way, but...you have awfully nice taste in clothes and wine for a military grunt." She smiled to show she didn't mean it hurtfully. To show she was curious, and would like to know more, but if he chose to pass it off as a joke, she'd respect his boundaries.

It was a risk. Some people took such remarks personally, and if Reb didn't see it for what it was, she'd apologize profusely.

To her relief, he laughed, his blush fading.

Between sips of his own wine, he admitted, "My grandfather drummed comportment into us boys from an early age, every chance he got. I can tell the price of a cigar to within pennies."

Reb knew his grandfather's world—but he also knew how to be generous and helpful.

An idea began to form in her mind. "And your suit? That isn't a boy's cut."

"This?" He raised one arm, his sleeve pulling back the perfect amount to show a sliver of pristine cuff fastened with a discreet onyx stud. "After I reupped in the Navy, the old man must've known I wasn't coming back to follow in his footsteps. But I returned to find a whole closet full of my-size robber-baron duds. He apparently finagled my measurements out of military records."

"Robber baron?" She laughed. "That's good. I call them sharks."

"Sharks." He gave her a rakish grin. "That's better. But maybe insulting the sharks. Sometimes, I think of them as a pack of wolves or feral dogs. Stealing bones. Attacking anyone not in the pack."

"Big dogs." She sighed.

"Why so serious all of a sudden?"

"That's my problem in a nutshell." She released another long breath.

He simply waited.

She wanted to stay silent. Her experience with the rest of the board told her he wouldn't understand her need to keep Landy's charities—Lovless Industries' heart and only soft spot—alive.

Hell, if the board even *suspected* her aims, it would actively suppress her, considering *any* soft spot a weakness.

She gazed into Reb's face, seeking an answer. *Tell him? Or not?* Faint lines fanned around his eyes, as if he laughed often. His gaze, waiting for her to speak, was patient. Kind, almost.

Yes, the board would try to suppress her or worse. *But Reb isn't one of them.* Despite the Lovless name, he was as much of an outsider as she.

Maybe she didn't stay silent because of that. Maybe it was the wine. Or maybe it was because Reb was Landy's grandson, and she missed Landy—*her* Landy, the kind old man—with a sudden, fierce longing.

"The board...they want me out," she said. Admitting weakness, top corporate mistake of all time. But something was pushing her to be honest with him, as honest as she'd been with his grandfather. "If I want to stay, I need to learn how to be a big dog."

The idea began to take form. *I need to be a big dog. Preston Hare won't help me, because he wants to be top dog himself. But Reb...he knows how to bark at the board and nip their heels until they do what he wants.*

"A big dog?" At first, Reb looked confused, and she feared she'd revealed herself for nothing. Then his confusion cleared to a look of intrigue. "Why?"

Because unless I can protect the charities, nobody will—and an old man's legacy will be stripped back to his youthful stupidity and greed.

Damn. To answer honestly, she'd have to admit that she'd worked, not just for Lovless Industries, but directly with his grandfather. Was still working for Landy, in a way.

That'll go over well. She was beginning to understand Reb didn't like Lovless Senior.

Business-wise, it was a bad move. Admitting the truth would anger her biggest ally.

But personally...if she was ever thinking of a relationship with this man, starting with lies was a bad idea.

A relationship? Wonder suffused her.

She pushed the feelings away and refocused on her original train of thought—his emphasis on team and trust meant if she wasn't honest with him and he found out later, she'd alienate him forever.

Still, she wriggled in her chair. The easiest choice was to keep quiet. Hope for the best.

Which felt wrong.

Elizabeth heaved a cleansing breath. "I have to tell you something."

"That doesn't sound good." He said it lightly, but his gaze had gone serious, and his body alarmingly still.

"Yes. Look, you and your grandfather didn't get along, right...?" Getting his silver bladed stare, she glanced away. "I used to work with him. Not just on the board, but directly with his charities."

When her gaze cut back to Reb's, she expected to see denial. Horror.

To her shock, he sat back with a half-smile, playing with the stem of his wine glass. "Well, that's a relief."

"A relief?"

"I'd seen some pictures of you and him on the Internet. When I was a boy, the old man marched a parade of younger and younger mistresses in front of my brothers and me. I worried... Well, I'm glad you two were just business partners."

Anger lit her blood. "How could you possibly think we were...I was...?" Although, how could he not? Her shoulders slumped. Before Landy's change of heart, he wasn't the nicest of men.

Realizing the relationship might have looked that way, not just to Reb, but to all the men on the board, the heat of her anger changed abruptly to embarrassment, rising hot up her neck into her face. "We were *never*... Reb, we were just allies on a hostile board. I took care of Landy's charities, and he protected me from the worst of the dog pack. But then..." She dropped her gaze, ashamed of what came next. "When Landy passed away, I still had the charities to protect. And I only had one possible ally on that board."

She stopped.

No. Courage.

She raised her gaze and firmly met Reb's. "Preston Hare and I wanted to maneuver you out of the captain's chair and put him into it. When it became obvious you weren't going to be maneuvered anywhere, well, Preston suggested I, um, romance you to get our way." She paused. Swallowed. Now would come the condemnation. The horror.

Instead, Reb surprised her again with a smile and nod. "Yes, that would have been effective." When she gasped, his smile grew. "Not the way you think. Because I know you wouldn't. You have character. Every time one of those assholes—pardon my language—one of those A-holes on the board tried to manipulate you, you resisted. Your natural excellence shines through."

Her hand rose to her cheek. It was flaming. "How you turned one of my biggest shames into a compliment is beyond me."

Their salads arrived as the sun set. The silver disk of the moon glowed brighter. A waiter came to each table to light candles, and another lit the torches ringing the terrace. The soft breeze played with a few tendrils of hair on her nape that had escaped her chignon, cooling the embarrassment from her heated skin.

With a heart lightened by her confessions, she started to hope. She raised her heavy silver fork to begin on her salad, trying to think of another topic of conversation. Such a shame to spoil the beauty of the evening with business.

"How you coped with the old bastard—sorry, old man—is beyond me." He forked up his own salad.

She heaved a breath. Yes, such a shame to spoil the beauty of the evening with business. Yet, that was all she and Reb had, wasn't it?

"Landy'd had a change of heart by the time I met him."

"Not possible. He was the meanest, most self-centered man I knew. And believe me, I knew him. He was at me constantly, trying to train me to take over his empire. Other kids get 'Early to bed and early to rise.' I got 'Don't get even, get revenge' and 'Always ask what's in it for you.' *The Art of War* and Machiavelli's *The Prince* were held up as my guidebooks."

"Ouch."

"I was shocked when I returned to administer his estate and found that Lovless Industries supports a dozen charities. That must've been you."

"No, Landy had already decided to fund good works on his own." *His grandfather had been training him to take over?* Her idea came back and sharpened. "But he had no idea how to pick charities or administer them. He hired me to help. But now..." She dropped her gaze and picked at her salad, wondering if she should break the spell of good wine and moonlit beach with her hopes, her fears.

Oh, hell. The mood was already broken, if it had ever been there to begin with.

She set down her fork and met his gaze. "Let me be blunt. I made a promise to Landy to keep those charities strong. But the board wants me out. The only way I can keep my promise to Landy is to run with the big dogs. To bark louder and bite harder than any of them." Her idea formed fully. "Reb, *you* can teach me how."

Chapter Ten

"You can teach me how."

Elizabeth waited, her breath held for Reb's response.

"Me?" Emotions chased across his face. Surprise, disbelief, dismay. "You want me to teach you to be as ruthless as those bastards? As ruthless as the grand bastard of them all?" He put down his fork with a solid thump. "No. You're empathetic and nurturing. I won't ruin that."

"It's the only way. If you turn me down, nobody will help me. I'll be fighting them alone...and I'll lose."

He seized her hands. "There has to be another solution. Barking with the dogs, swimming with the sharks... whatever your analogy, that's not you. Trying to be a bastard would hurt you, the *real* you." He squeezed her hands for emphasis before releasing them.

"Hurt *me?*" She laughed in disbelief. "*You're* the one who made me his right-hand shark."

She dared to snatch his hands back. His were big, warm. Callused. Strong. Hands that knew how to work, and how to pleasure a woman... With a shiver, she recalled herself to her purpose.

"While Landy was still alive, he protected me, so I never learned how to defend myself. Now, that's coming back to bite me...if you'll pardon the pun."

"*I* can protect you—"

"While you're here. But you're not staying, are you?"

He flinched, all the answer she needed.

"And since you're not staying...I *must* be able to protect myself. I need to be a big dog on the board. Bigger, harder, and meaner than any of them."

His gaze slid away. "Let's not talk about this now. We're here to have dinner. Let's eat."

The rest of the meal, while excellent, was subdued. She tried to turn the conversation a couple times back to helping her beat the board, but he deftly avoided each gambit.

So, she was surprised when, instead of making excuses after coffee, he escorted her to her room.

Outside her door, she turned to him. His gaze was zeroed on her lips.

Is he going to kiss me?

All thoughts of training fell away. Moonlight, fine food and wine, and the delight of a handsome, attentive man collided inside her as "business or pleasure" crystallized...

Into *pleasure.*

Her pulse beat faster, her lips throbbing with the rhythm of her heart. She raised her fingertips to his chest and leaned into him, eyelids closing, signaling her desire to be kissed. To explore the attraction simmering between them. To breathe on it and perhaps kindle it into more. To open the door to her room, stumble in still lost in each other, heat rising between them, seeking completion in the oldest way known to woman and man...

The oldest way. She remembered Preston Hare mouthing those words, wanting her to use sex to seduce the heir.

Her eyelids shot open, and she parted her lips to refuse.

Reb's face was *right there.* His eyes were closed, lashes black against his chiseled cheeks, his lips so close to hers she felt the warmth of his breath on her skin.

The sensitive skin of her lips, blood rushing hard through them now.

Doubt was lost in that rush of blood, whooshing in her ears and pooling heavy and hot in her pelvis.

His mouth touched hers.

Need burst inside her like the pop of champagne as his mouth claimed her. His breath mingled with hers, minty with undertones of brandy and coffee, and she leaned into him.

He groaned softly. His arms came around her to pull her closer. Beneath her flattened palms his chest muscles moved intriguingly. She'd admired his physique, but that wasn't nearly the same as touching him.

And tasting him. His tongue slid between her lips, and her whole body went haywire.

He cupped her face in one big, warm, confident palm. Holding her for a deeper, more intimate kiss.

She opened to him, wanting even more. Minute shivers of desire cascaded through her.

He clasped her body to his so firmly her whole body flushed with the need to feel him pressed to her just like this—but naked.

Her searing, immediate response to him told her he'd be the lover that made the others fade into history. The man she'd compare any future lovers with.

The one she wanted above all others...

"Did you seduce him yet?"

"Any way you have to."

...and the one she could never have, thanks to Preston Hare.

She groaned. Why now? But the memory had intervened. Regret invading every cell, she pulled back. "Reb..."

He groaned in response but released her.

Elizabeth opened her eyes. Beyond the thudding of her heart in her ears, she heard his rasp of breath. His nostrils were white. He'd been as affected by that kiss as she.

"Reb...this is what Preston wanted."

"Honest to the last." His gaze searched hers. Then he stepped back, rubbing his nape with a sigh. "Elizabeth...what you said before is true. I'm not staying, and you need to be able to protect yourself."

"So you'll teach me?"

"I still don't think it's a good idea. I had hoped..."

I had hoped... What? That the board would have a sudden change of heart? That *he'd stay* with her? She hung on his next words.

But instead of finishing the thought, he inhaled as if girding himself for a fight. When he exhaled, he was completely relaxed. Ready. Like in the alley before he'd fought the muggers. "I respect your wishes. What the old man taught me isn't nice at all, but if you're sure...?"

Am I sure? Her body still sang from the press of his, and the last thing she wanted to do was talk business. But she needed to protect the charities and wanted to make a difference in the world. Learning to fight the board was the best way. Pleasure was a luxury she didn't have. "Yes. I'm sure."

"All right. I'll teach you. Meet me on the roof tomorrow."

He turned and strode away. She shivered, as if, despite the short time he'd been in her life, she'd gotten used to the heat of his big body and suddenly felt cold and alone. *Ridiculous.* Resolutely, she turned, unlocked her door, and went into her room to strip off her date self and prepare for shark training tomorrow.

Chapter Eleven

The next morning, Reb paced the rooftop garden in turmoil, waiting for Elizabeth. He stared at the sun, barely risen, still softened by first-morning haze. That would burn off soon enough, revealing what a bastard the tropical sun could be.

He was afraid the same thing would happen to Elizabeth.

A click sounded behind him. He spun. She came hesitantly from the exit hut onto the roof. The lush foliage paled to him beside the sight of her plump rosy lips, her sparkling eyes, the soft sweep of her golden hair.

Why had he ever thought he didn't like cool blondes? She was exquisite.

And it was his job to break her.

He strode toward her. "We'll start with assertiveness training. I'm going to get in your face. I want you to repeat 'Back off.' Like you did in the alley attack, but over and over. A broken record. Hard. Got it?"

She glanced around. "Won't we disturb people?"

"Nobody's up here. I reserved it for an hour. The greenery will absorb the worst of our yelling." He hardened his stance. "Get off the board, woman."

Her eyes narrowed. "Back off."

"Good," he said in a normal tone. "Now again, but put some air behind it. Really fill your lungs." He stepped into her personal space and prepared to yell. Her perfume wafted into his nose, her heat touched him, and instead, he had to clamp down hard on the memory of the last time they were this close. When he was kissing her soft, sweet lips... "Get off the board."

Some yell, Lovless.

"Back *off*." Her gaze flared.

Teach her right. "You're a frill. A *liability*." He crowded her with his body, flinching when she took an involuntary step back. But she'd wanted this, and he'd help her the only way she'd accept. "You're damaging the board."

Her shoulders squared. Gaze blazing, she took a threatening step toward him. "Back off!"

A spark of pride warmed him. Maybe this wouldn't damage her. Being assertive was a good thing, right? It had helped her survive in the alley, and it'd help her survive in the boardroom.

They practiced for half an hour that way, Elizabeth growing in confidence.

Then she said, "Okay, I'm ready for the next step."

"I don't understand." But he did.

"Your grandfather didn't just teach you to be assertive, right?"

Yes. The old bastard had taught him to be cunning and mean.

She asked me to teach her what he taught me.

"Come on, Reb. How can I learn if you hold back?"

"I'm not holding back. You just don't understand—"

"No, I *don't* understand," she exclaimed, hands waving in exasperation. "How'd your grandfather give you that tough carapace? I need to be just as tough. Tougher!" When he still hesitated, she yelled, "*Show* me, dammit."

Reb took the next, awful step. "You don't have what it takes." And then he used the roughest, toughest derogative term he could think of. His voice shook using it. Bitch.

Even without force behind the word, her pupils constricted in pain, and her face drained of blood.

He wanted to call the word back, to enfold her in his arms and take away her hurt forever...

Then her jaw tightened so hard he could hear her teeth clack. Her gaze narrowed like a machete. "You bastard. You think you know me? Back off. Back the hell *off!*" She shoved him away.

He let her move him a step, swallowing a lump of regret. He'd known it'd be painful, teaching her what his grandfather taught him. *How* his grandfather had taught him. But she'd wanted this.

Damn. It was killing him.

He blew an aggravated breath. "I'm sorry, but this is the next step. Beyond assertive is absolute control. You control your opponent by threat, by force, by getting under his skin. Any way you can."

"That's what Preston Hare said," she whispered. "Any way. Is that how your grandfather taught you?"

"Yes. Threat and force, verbal or physical. And getting under your opponent's skin...that's the worst."

She swallowed hard. "Show me."

His grandfather had taken him to the roof of his New York skyscraper. Showed him the street below. The cars scuttled like beetles, the people like ants. *"They're sheep,*

Landon. They want to be told what to do. Go on, order them around. You're giving them what they want."

As a boy, he hadn't known better, and he'd tried his grandfather's techniques.

And they'd *worked.* He'd felt fierce satisfaction and believed the old man was right. A hero.

Until one time, he destroyed his opponent—and right before the other boy walked away, Reb saw the pain in the boy's eyes.

Yes. The techniques worked.

But what was the cost? Pain. Suffering. A price paid by other people. He saw that. But another cost revealed itself only as he got older.

The cost to his own soul.

"Reb, show me," she said again.

"Are you sure—?"

"Yes." She squared her shoulders and blew out a breath, as if getting ready to go three rounds in the ring. "If you don't, Exetor or one of the hatchet men will. Do it."

"Right." He hated this. "So, how'd seducing the heir go last night? Did you get him to do what you wanted?"

She paled. Her chest stopped its rise and fall for a second. When she started breathing again, she was panting, like she'd taken a physical hit.

Her pain was like a sword to his gut. Thrust deep, twisted for extra anguish. Why had she asked him for this, damn it? "Come on, Elizabeth, stab at me in return." He waited, watching her gaze wildly searching his face.

"W-would your grandfather have...? W-would he have waited for you to recover?"

No. He'd have goaded me until I broke.

Reb swallowed a lump of infinite regret. He hated this— but he hated worse the idea of her defenseless after he left.

For her. To armor her when I'm gone.

"If kissing the heir doesn't work, maybe you should try spreading your legs for him. That'll get you what you want."

"Right." Her eyes clenched shut a moment. Then she opened them and they blazed. "Screw you, Lovless."

It was better than the pale, hurt look. He hoped like hell that meant he was doing the right thing.

She stalked up to him, anger almost a force emanating from her body. "The heir didn't take much convincing, if you really want to know. I think he's been in the desert too long." She nailed him in the eye. "He's desperate for any kind of connection."

His mouth dried suddenly, any response dying. God. He'd known it'd be painful, teaching her to be hard, but it was worse. He wanted to shrivel into an insect.

And they were just starting. What would happen to her? To him?

What would happen to them?

He shied away from that thought. There was no *them*.

But he'd thought the cost to his soul was the worst thing he'd ever see. Now he saw something far worse, something beyond any horror he could have even imagined.

He saw the cost to *Elizabeth's* soul. And it was his fault.

*   *   *

Reb met again with Elizabeth that evening, after working on the house. He wished she hadn't insisted. But she had, and she continued to insist. He trained her morning and night, and it was harder for him every damned time.

And here he'd thought getting the board to cooperate would be tough. Instead, as the week progressed, the members dug into the project with relish. But Elizabeth, sweet Elizabeth...she was changing before his eyes.

At first, she pulled on self-centered meanness like an ill-fitting coat. Then she became more comfortable with it and wore it with confidence.

And then the poison of it began to seep into her bones.

The fifth morning, she stepped out of the exit hut and immediately lashed out at him, without provocation, without a moment's hesitation.

"You spineless bastard. You think you're such a hero, don't you? Big SEAL, fighting wars. But the biggest, most important war of all is going on right here, right now. And you're running out on it."

Going for the jugular.

"Okay." He breathed through his pain, and breathed again. She'd caught him off-guard and in a soft, vulnerable place. "You're right."

Something flickered in her eyes, some hidden hurt, some secret empathy. She opened her mouth, maybe to apologize or try to soothe him.

Then, slowly, her lips closed. Her stance firmed and her gaze hardened.

He nodded, not feeling terribly steady. He'd done it. He'd done as she'd asked, and turned her into a soulless shark. Yes, it would protect her when he was gone, but what was left of his own soul shriveled in agony. "You know what? Enough. You're ready. Let's move on to exactly how you're going to secure your place as head of the board."

Chapter Twelve

"Head of the board?" Elizabeth felt like Reb had punched her. And that was despite her skin being yards thicker than when she'd first started. Was this part of her training? Her heart thudded in her chest. "I wanted to bark like a big dog, not lead the pack."

He gave her a wan smile. "If you were the typical dog, you could. But as a poodle, I'm afraid the only way to make sure you have *any* power is for you to have *all* the power. You have to be boss."

"Well…" She considered it. As boss, she'd never be threatened again. As boss, she could make sure Landy's charities never ran out of money. "How?"

"Tomorrow night is the final board meeting, the one where I was going to gauge how much progress they'd made, compassion-wise. You're going to head that meeting instead."

"I'm not chairperson."

"You don't have to be. My brothers and I have controlling shares—I'll give you proxy. You'll have the entire Lovless brothers' voting interest behind you."

"But what if the board doesn't listen?"

"Appeal to their sense of self-preservation—fire someone. I guarantee they'll listen, then."

She sucked in a shocked breath. "I can't do that."

"Why not? Frankly, I was planning to, if they hadn't made progress. I was ready to retire them *all* and start fresh."

Shocked already, she could only stare.

He took her hands, as he had at dinner that first night. As he hadn't done since. "You can do this Elizabeth. I have faith in you."

His grip was firm, reassuring, warm. She thawed. "I can do this," she echoed. Then, strengthened by his touch, she ventured, "After this is over..."

Reb was kind and thoughtful and sexy as hell. And even in the midst of his worst training taunts, he stopped to encourage her, to reassure her. He cared about her.

More, she'd seen the pain in his gaze every time he hurt her. What wondrous strength he had, that a man had whipped him as hard or harder for years, and he'd ended up compassionate and caring in spite of it?

So she dared, "After this is over...could we stay in touch? Be friends? Maybe...maybe more?"

His smile twisted. "Elizabeth, I think I'm falling for you."

She gave him a tremulous smile in return. His words were sweet music, but his pained expression added a sour note. "Why do you make that sound like a bad thing?"

He released her hands with a sigh. Checked his watch. He waved a hand toward a bench beside a potted palm tree. "My life growing up was...complicated. One part was completely normal. My brothers and I squabbled, my parents loved us all equally and wished we'd all be quiet equally." He lowered himself onto the bench, staring into the rising sun.

She smiled at the thought of a small Reb, making a racket with his brothers while his parents looked fondly on. She settled herself by his side. "And the complication?"

"My grandfather—he wanted my mother gone. 'Thanks for the heirs, but you're a bad influence on my son.' Truth was, my dad wasn't cut out for high-pressure boardrooms. He loved growing plants. He might have made a decent farmer, but never the prince of business my grandfather expected him to be. And then, after my parents died...my grandfather turned his expectations on me."

"I'm so sorry. How old were you?"

"Twelve. The next five years were hell. He'd always pushed his views on us, but as our guardian, there was no squabbling and there certainly was no love. He was the reason I left home, the reason I joined the Navy."

"Because you didn't like him?"

"Because he would have *made me just like him*." His gaze snapped to her and he unleashed a frustrated snarl. Immediately, he shook his head and looked away. "I'm not being clear. Elizabeth, my grandfather was lauded as a king of business, but I saw him for what he really was." His eyes turned toward the sun, blazing with reflected light and fury. "A man whose greed and conniving killed my parents."

She gasped. "You can't mean it."

"I do." His mouth tightened. "Always scheming to force my mother out of our lives, to get my father to 'man up' as he said. Going around her to pound the weakness out of us. But the worst..." The blaze in his eyes died, and his shoulders slumped.

Her heart beat in pain for him. Whatever his grandfather had done, it was truly horrible. Anguish drew harsh lines in Reb's face, a muscle jumping in his clenching jaw.

She put her arms around him. "Tell me?"

His ribs expanded under her embrace as he took a deep, unhappy breath. "H-he tried...oh, God. He tried to get control of us boys by declaring Mom unfit."

Pain for him cut through her. "Reb," she whispered and just held him.

His body trembled in her arms, wracked with unshed tears. Her own eyes welled hot in distress for him.

"The old man was trying to remake me in his own image even before my parents died. Once he had sole control, every moment was pressure to change." He pulled in another tortured breath. "I know you want to be a shark, and that you think it's a good thing. I tried to respect that. I've turned you into the biggest, meanest shark there is. I knew just how to do it because my grandfather did it to me. But Libet..." The endearment was almost a hiccup.

She rubbed his shoulders until he swallowed hard and started to pull away from her. She didn't want to let him go, not in his strangely fragile state. But he'd respected her needs, and it was her turn to respect his. She relaxed her hold and let him pull out of her arms.

"Elizabeth..." He sat away from her.

"I think I like Libet better." She tried to laugh.

"I vowed *never* to be like him. I can't..." His gaze was anguished. "I *can't* be with anyone like that." In those pained eyes, she read the rest of it.

Now that you're *like that—I can't be with* you.

His eyes flicked away. Her gut chilled.

Softly, he said, "I just can't."

He creaked to his feet like an old man.

Elizabeth sat on the bench, shivering, as he walked away. His back was as straight and his shoulders as square as always, but she read his sorrow in every muscle and sinew.

Her question: *I know you're leaving but could we be friends—maybe more?*

His answer: *I just can't.*

Her heart broke.

Chapter Thirteen

That evening, Elizabeth dressed with care in her black power suit and chunky gold jewelry. Four inch heels, the kind that boomed when she walked.

Outside, she was all fierce power.

Inside, she was frozen.

Can we be more?

I can't.

She used her cold wretchedness like a sword of ice, hacking her tender heart unmercifully until she bled—and using the blood like a berserker to stoke her rage.

Cold fury drove her stalk into that board meeting. She entered the room like she owned it, ready to use her anger and resentment to get her way however—*any way*—she had to.

She was momentarily surprised to see the men, not sitting like a ring of wolves around the table, but in clumps, chatting. Overhearing a couple groups as she made her way to the power chair at the center, she was even more surprised they were discussing the good they'd done. Those cranky, self-serving old men were wondering if they might carry some of the things they'd learned into the boardroom.

With the right leadership, this board might truly change.

Can we be more?

I can't.

She was alone against the sharks. *Screw it.* Her turn to be selfish.

Elizabeth took the power position and rapped on the table for attention. "You know why you're all here."

"Where's young Mr. Lovless?" Exetor Senior's tone was almost jovial.

"He won't be coming. Hell, he's leaving anyway, going back to his SEAL unit. I have voting proxy for his block, and that of his brothers."

The meeting went rapidly downhill after that.

Backs went up. Greed came back online. One of the hatchet men tried to bury his meat cleaver in her. She spun it from his grasp and used it to chop his attempt in two. A young buck tried to shout over her and take credit for her ideas. She snarled him down.

Then Preston Hare tut-tutted. "Elizabeth, you're obviously stressed. Women like you aren't meant for this kind of pressure. Let me take over for you."

She fired his ass.

Rolex looked shocked. His father, old Exetor Senior, looked *intrigued.*

Damn him.

Swimming with the sharks, she knew she had to be a shark. She'd worried all along that she'd fail.

Reb's training, learned at the feet of the best—or worst—shark there was, meant she didn't fail. She succeeded.

Succeeded so well she reduced the board to a handful of sniveling five year olds in ten minutes.

She strode out of there having turned most of them to ash—and having impressed the worst of them.

Returning to her room, she shed her business suit and ordered room service champagne and caviar to celebrate.

And hated herself the whole time.

She popped the cork, downed a glass...and another. Waiting for the hot flush of success, or at least the warm fizz of alcohol.

Only cold inside. Numb.

Damn it, drinking alone wasn't going to get her anywhere. Donning a simple sundress, she went down to the executive bar and marched straight to the biggest booth in the farthest corner.

The hatchet men already there saw her coming and scrabbled to vacate.

A grim laugh bubbled up inside her for a moment. Then...nothing.

She sat and ordered scotch, straight. Board members crawled up to her one by one like dogs with their tails between their legs to congratulate her.

Numb, she listened to them and drank scotch. Numb, except for the self-hatred in her heart.

Her eyes itched, but she knew better than to give into the tears sobbing in her chest.

Into that abyss of her soul, Reb appeared like a warm beacon of light—or an avenging angel.

"Celebrating?" He slid onto the bench opposite with a smile, probably sympathetic, but Elizabeth was too frozen to tell.

"Mourning."

"Right. Let's get out of here."

"I want to drink." *I need to drink.*

"Yes. I know a better place.

He led her outside to a sleek motorcycle and handed her a helmet—his. Mounting bare-headed himself, he waited until she got the thing on her skull and was up behind him before kicking the stand and rolling away.

The moment they were out of sight of the resort, the board, those *condemning eyes,* she broke down sobbing. Well, hell, nobody could see her in this helmet anyway. The crying made her whole face hot and humid in the can of the brain bucket.

Briefly, he gripped one of her arms where it wrapped around him, as if encouraging her to let it out.

With her arms embracing his solid strength, the rumble of the motorcycle a comforting drone in her ears, she let herself cry.

Reb drove around for minutes, hours, days...she lost track of time. But as she hiccupped the last of her tears, he came to a halt and stopped the engine. She felt him lean the bike onto its stand beneath her. She dismounted, unsteady on her sandaled feet.

He had a paper napkin waiting for her the moment she lifted the helmet.

"How did you know...?"

"Sweetheart. We've been working together, under pressure, all week. Both on the housing site and in the rooftop garden. I know you by now."

She wiped away the worst of her tears and saw...the resort hotel. "We didn't go anywhere."

"We got away. That was the important thing. Now we're going somewhere safe." He took her by the hand and led her in through a back way to a freight elevator.

"How did you find this?"

"Bad habit. I did recon when we first arrived."

A tiny laugh burbled up, one that she would've thought impossible before. "Where are we going?"

"The most private bar there is." The elevator stopped at the top. "My penthouse."

He led her into the spacious suite. Gorgeous carpeting and exotic tile were accented by rich wood the color of maple syrup.

"You're safe here, Elizabeth." He led her by the hand to a plush sofa. As she sank into the cushions, he went to a polished wood bar. After a few clinks and *glugs*, he returned with two tumblers of amber liquid and ice.

Her earlier scotches seemed to have burned away. She grabbed one drink, tossed it down in a single gulp, then reached for the other.

He smiled quizzically at her as he handed over the glass. "I guess you can have mine." He settled in beside her, thigh touching hers. "Tell me."

"It was awful, Reb. They were talking about how the homebuilding experience changed them, and I—*I shut them down*. Kicked them right back into shark mode."

"I'm sure it wasn't that bad."

"It was *worse*. I was angry and hateful." She looked at him, and his form swam in her sight. "I f-fired Preston Hare."

"Good." He brushed a drying thumb under her eyes. "Hare *is* a bit of a dick."

She gave a watery laugh. "But dickish enough to deserve firing?"

"You did it to win."

"Yes. I'd determined to win any way I had to, no matter how awful it made me feel, but..." She had hardly admitted the worst to herself. Here, in Reb's private space, with his warmth so near, she felt safe enough to whisper, "Reb—I enjoyed it." She peeked up at him. Expecting condemnation. *Hoping* for absolution.

But he said, "I expect you did."

She flinched. Her gaze dropped, her shoulders sagged, and her whole being shriveled.

His finger slid under her chin, warm and firm, and turned her face up to him. "Elizabeth, you're human and competitive. You enjoy winning. That's natural and fine."

"Not me!" But she had. Something inside her broke. "I thought."

"You enjoy winning—but you don't enjoy seeing others suffer." He paused. "Except for Preston Hare. Him being such a dick."

That goosed a laugh out of her, more of a hiccup. Then she sobered. "But the rest weren't being dicks, not when I first came in. You'd hoped for that, didn't you? Hoped the experience of building a house, a *home,* would change the board for the better."

"Or at least *start* to change them, yes."

"They can." She grabbed his hands and tried to communicate all her needs, her fears, her desires, with her gaze. "I really believe, with the right leadership, they can become what you want them to be. But not with me as chairperson." She swallowed hard. "Not if I continue like this."

She didn't know what she expected him to say. *I'll make it all better, Elizabeth. I'll stay. Be here for you.*

Be here with *you.*

But he went silent. And then he slid his hands from hers.

Leaving her cold again. No, colder than before.

Chapter Fourteen

Reb sat beside Elizabeth, her thigh warm against his, his thoughts in turmoil.

He'd let go of her hands to have the separation to think. He was silent to make sure when he did talk, what he said was best for them both.

Her shoulders hunched, and she seemed to fold in on herself.

Damn it, he'd had years to come to grips with his grandfather's sadistic training. She'd had a week.

Her lower lip started quivering. She was hurting and vulnerable, and he'd just unintentionally abandoned her.

Okay, he'd have to work through it with her and hope for the best. He snatched her hands, and was rewarded with her body relaxing. "When I came home, all I wanted to do was leave again. Go back to my SEAL team."

"To the men who understand you."

"Yes, but more. To escape my grandfather's legacy. Being a soulless monster was the worst thing I thought I could face. But trying to turn you into that same thing..." His grip tightened on her hands. Her return grip was almost painfully tight. "Seeing you angry and vengeful was... Bad enough. But seeing you like this..." The carapace of greed crushing the sensitive soul beneath, the pain lancing through her hurt eyes, crying for help... "It's like falling on the IED all over again, but this time without the vest. It's tearing me apart."

"I'm sorry," she whispered.

That helped. "Elizabeth, I know what you need me to do. You need me to stay and protect you. But what that will make me..." He shook his head and looked away. Him or her. One of them had to step into his grandfather's cruel shoes.

His will solidified. He met her gaze. "Doesn't matter. If I have to be the monster, I will."

"Oh, Reb." Her palm slid onto his jaw, tilting his head toward her. She kissed him.

Her breath was fresh from the motorcycle ride. Warm and sweet from the alcohol. Her lips were pillow soft, moving like silk on his.

His desire surged and crashed within him, tightening every muscle into instant readiness. He palmed her head in return and deepened the kiss. Her mouth was swollen, her breath hot. From desire or tears? But she'd started it. Maybe she wasn't in a place she could really enjoy sex but needed the comfort of physical intimacy?

He wanted her badly, so bad he almost let it be enough.

But sex as a palliative—any man could give her that. Any man could comfort her when she was emotionally wrought and vulnerable. Any man would do if she was just drunk and horny. He didn't want their lovemaking to be an act she could have with any man.

When he and Elizabeth came together, he wanted it to be spurred by the passion that only existed between her and him.

Stunned, he realized he loved her, the kind of love that gave up mere sex for a closer intimacy.

"Elizabeth," he muttered against her mouth. "You're overwrought. We shouldn't..."

She took advantage of his parted lips and thrust her tongue into his mouth. It was like a bomb of lust to his groin.

He groaned. "I'm trying to do the right thing."

"Then take me to bed."

"Now isn't the time—"

"Now is exactly the time." She grabbed his face and pulled him back so he could see the determination in her gaze. "Your concern for me only makes me want you more. Take me to bed, Reb. Take me now and help me forget the horror of that boardroom."

He studied her face. Reckless need blazed in her eyes. Desire glowed in her cheeks. And her mouth...

"Please, Reb. Don't make me ask again."

Tight. Thin. Beneath the need, the desire, he saw her pain. Her hidden fear.

Fear that he was rejecting her.

In the end, it was that which decided him. He swept her into his arms, lifted her, and stood.

* * *

Elizabeth clung to Reb's neck as he carried her, kissing his cheek, his jaw, his ear, everything she could reach. Trying to tell him how much she needed this.

He laid her on the bed, released her, and tried to straighten, maybe to remove his clothes.

But she clung even tighter. Arms wrapped around him like a second skin, she came onto her knees to stay with him, fastening onto his mouth with a kiss. But him, naked, was a good idea. Without unlocking her arms, she tried to wrestle the hem of his shirt from his pants.

Chuffing a laugh, he gave in, diving onto the bed and flipping her on top of him.

She woofed air. It was like landing on a stone slab. He was solid muscle.

The rasp of her zipper was followed by her sundress loosening. Suddenly impatient, she sat straight on his hips, grinding her panties into all that was glorious, and stripped the dress over her head. She'd worn no bra and her breasts bounced free.

He gaped, eyes glued to her. She grinned savagely down at him. He probably wasn't surprised often, and she liked it. To keep him off kilter, she bent until her nipple touched his mouth and undulated, teasing his lips open.

Almost automatically, his mouth closed around the tip of her breast. He began suckling, the tugging sparking a thrill of urgency through her. Her body shivered with response. Hands trembling, she peeled off his shirt then reached between them to undo his belt.

"This would be easier," he said between sucks, "if you let me up."

"I don't want easy." She paused wrestling with the belt to cup his face in both hands. "I want feeling. I want touch."

His gaze flew up to hers, and she knew he could read her deepest desire. Not just sex. Yes, she needed to lose herself in his embrace. But more, she simply needed his embrace. His arms around her, holding her tight, never letting go.

He groaned and pulled her into a passionate kiss. Her breasts pressed to his naked chest, the sheen of perspiration prickling between them. His panted breaths rubbed the hair on his belly against her. She squirmed on his hips, his zipper rising beneath her.

"I-if you'd let me," he panted. "I could get my pants off."

"No time." She thrust her tongue between his lips, impaling him with her need, while she fussed between her thighs with his buckle and snap and zipper. She wrestled the cloth open just enough to feel the rounded hardness rising between. "Oh, heavens." She closed her fist around the top of his erection.

He gasped into her mouth. "Yeah."

She rose slightly on her knees and hooked the crotch of her panties aside to lever him into position. He took advantage of the moment to wrestle his pants down onto his thighs.

So when she sat, it was with him boldly in place. She eased down onto him. Each inch made him—and her—hiss with pleasure. When she sat again on his hips, she was utterly filled.

His hands pressed against her breasts. His gaze snared hers, the silver of his eyes blazing. "Elizabeth. I've never felt this way. You're amazing."

She wanted to stare into those passionate eyes forever. But urgency seized her, and she had to move. Her hips beat once, twice, against his.

He groaned from the pit of his being. "I have to kiss you." Arms wrapping around her, he cupped the back of her head and pressed her toward him. She went eagerly, mouth opening to receive his tongue. He began to move beneath her, tongue and hips thrusting boldly into her, less in possession than in joining.

As if he needed to connect as deeply as she.

She wrapped arms around his broad shoulders and rolled her hips and thrust her tongue in turn, feeling the joining going deeper and deeper. As deep as her heart. As deep as her soul. As they met each other thrust for thrust, her passion rose to dizzying, almost fearful heights. She cried out, awed by what was coming.

"Elizabeth. *Love.*"

The word pushed her over. She soared into the chasm, tumbling with wave after wave of bone-deep pleasure.

He clasped her almost desperately to his hot, damp body, thrust one last time, and began to shudder in climax.

Clinging to him, enfolded by him, she rode his release with little pulls of her hips, drawing her own pleasure out. When it was finally done, she felt remade. Clean. Brand-new.

Beneath her, Reb's hard muscles relaxed. She eased off him, about to get off the bed to find the bathroom.

His arms loosened but didn't open. Reluctant herself to lose skin-to-skin touch, she eased in beside him and nestled close.

*   *   *

Reb lay pressed to Elizabeth's soft flesh, stunned. That had been...well... Sex was always good for him, but this had been so much more. His thoughts drifted as his body cooled into profound relaxation.

Not sex. Lovemaking. His lids slid shut. Moving in perfect sync.

She snuggled into him. He sighed, almost asleep. In perfect sync, body and soul.

Like...

His eyes flew open in shock. "Elizabeth."

"Mmm?"

"I think I know what we can do."

"What we did was just fine." She murmured it through a smile.

"About Lovless Industries."

Her eyes slit open, not pleased. "Can't we ever have pleasure without business?"

"Sorry. This is important. I think. I hope. Elizabeth, our lovemaking just now...you and I are in sync, like my SEAL team."

"That's good, right?"

"I wanted to leave because there's no team here for me to rely on, only my grandfather's legacy of bitterness and mistrust."

"You said that before."

"No team—unless we build one. What do you say? You and me."

She blinked a moment. Then frowning, she eased herself to sit. Stared down at him. "A team of two?"

"Your charities, my grandfather's last, best self—they need nurturing. Protecting. I can protect them, and hey, you're nurturing."

"You Dick, me Jane?" Her gaze turned flinty. "I can protect them now, too."

"Yes, you can." He pushed himself to sit beside her. "We both can do both, but with two of us, neither of us can do both all the time." *I don't have to be my grandfather all the time.* "We're best as a team. Right?"

She didn't answer. Or rather, her answer was to swing her legs over the side of the bed and get up.

His heart fell, watching her hunt for her clothes, watching her dress. "Elizabeth?"

She strode to the door then tilted a tight half-smile back at him. "You make a solid point, Lovless. But it's too close to letting Landy protect me, all over again. Let me think it through."

Reb smiled and nodded, but inside he was dying. Bad enough he'd offered the thing he thought she wanted, his protection, and she'd rejected it.

But what he'd really been offering her was himself. A possible future. A *them*.

She'd just walked out on him. On them. As the door shut behind her, its hollow thud echoed the hollowness in his chest.

Chapter Fifteen

Elizabeth returned to her room on the fourth floor feeling much more in control. Feeling fabulous, actually.

Which was part of the problem. She didn't want to say yes to Reb's idea of a team because it was a good idea—it was—she wanted to say yes to those gorgeous blue eyes and handsome face. To the man.

Needing to talk things over, she called her friends. Despite the late hour, she didn't think she'd wake them. Harper had a computer hacker's late-night affinity, and Ainsley often worked into the small hours of the night on her news stories.

Of the three of them, Elizabeth was the one who usually made the morning coffee.

She paced the small room until Ainsley answered. "Elizabeth? Why are you awake this late, hon? What's wrong?"

That put a smile on her face. "You know me so well. I have something I need to talk out. But first, how are you and Harper? Fido okay?"

"We're great. We got Fido a catnip mouse. Man, he loves that crazy thing. Well, if biting and clawing and shaking it dead count as loving."

"Ainsley!" she cried in mock-despair. "I leave poor Fido alone with you two reprobates for a week, and you hook him on drugs? *Tsk, tsk.*"

Her friend laughed. "So, what's the thing you need to talk about?"

"Well...it's complicated." She sank onto the room's corner chair, trying to figure out where to start.

Ainsley waited a couple beats before saying, "Not quite ready? All right, I'll talk to fill in. You know Lovless McHottie has a brother, right?"

"Lovless McHottie...?" A helpless giggle bubbled up inside her, straightening her in the chair. "You mean Reb?"

"Yeah, well, Clan McHottie bred true with brother number two. Lucas Lovless is a billionaire in his own right, in the entertainment industry. Rich as sin, sporting a new supermodel each week, both car and fashion. Charming— and shallow. Or at least that's what we're supposed to think."

"What?"

"I've discovered it's a *cover*. I don't know as a cover for what, but it's got to be some nefarious activity, right? If he supported orphanages in his spare time, he wouldn't need to cover that up. I'm doing an exposé. I wrangled an invite to his exclusive house party next weekend. I'll dig up the dirt then!"

"Congratulations." Then she thought of Reb. If Lucas Lovless was half as smart and tough as his brother, he wouldn't take Ainsley's digging into his private life lying down. The thought pushed her to her feet and into pacing. "Be careful, will you?"

"You betcha. You ready to dish?"

Her pacing took her to the mirror. She stopped and stared at herself, at her glowing eyes and bed-rumpled hair. "Umm…"

"Okay, I'll guess. My investigative nose is, of course, top-notch. It's late—so you did the deed with Lovless McHottie—but it's still hours before breakfast-in-bed time, so while the deed was far-out fabulous, he threw you a curve ball."

Elizabeth didn't know whether to laugh or cry. "Your news nose is exceptional."

Haltingly, she told Ainsley everything. Her pacing took her to the closet, where her severe suits hung. She fingered one, feeling the rough linen as she spoke, finishing her story with, "I allowed Landy to protect me from the board, and I nearly lost everything. Now Reb is suggesting something similar."

"*Similar* isn't 'the same.' I know that because I'm a professional wordsmith."

Even in the midst of her serious trouble, Ainsley made her smile.

Like Reb did.

Her hand moved to hover over her little black dress. "I need to be tough—"

"Elizabeth, you *are* tough."

"I wasn't before Reb." Her hand dropped.

"No, you were—when you needed to be. With Old Man Lovless, you didn't need to be. When he died, you did."

"But I wasn't tough enough." She paused. Yes, some part of her had enjoyed finally winning against the sharks. But in the end… "I broke, proving I'll never be completely ruthless."

"Because tough isn't your strength. Your huge capacity for caring is your strength."

Snorting, Elizabeth turned away from the closet. "Caring doesn't buy me votes in the boardroom."

"It does, actually, but not by itself."

"I don't understand." But she turned back to the closet, where her suits and dress hung side by side. Her gut knew.

"You want to swim with the sharks, right? Sharks swim with sharks—but humans can swim with the sharks, too, with a shark cage."

"A *what...?* Are you suggesting I use Reb as a diving cage?" Then she snapped her fingers. "No. I can use a *team* as a shark cage. A bigger team than Reb and me. So neither of us is in the sole role of hard-ass—so we don't have to be the cage—all the time."

"You're a bright lady. You'll be protected by the team—and so will everyone else. That's part of teamwork. But you have to head it."

"Me? No. Reb's the leader. He's a SEAL. He's Landy's heir."

"Sure. But the charities are *your* babies. Cowgirl up, lady. You're the best one to put this particular team together."

Her emotions churned; pain, fear, shame, and hope ignited and boiled over. "But what if I get it wrong again?" She'd been such a *good* shark. Too good.

"That's what your team is for, to keep you from going dark-side. Like the three of us. We're late and you're early, we split the rent so none of us have to pay too much—we balance each other out, yeah?"

"Yes."

"Put together a team like that."

As Elizabeth hung up, all her feelings, fear and hurt and shame over what she'd done still roiled inside.

But hope eclipsed them all.

Pulling a pad of paper from her messenger bag, she listed her goals into the long night. Then, as the clock ticked past three, she began to map strategies.

She could have called Reb and talked it over with him. Need goosed her to reach for the phone several times. But that would undermine the point. If she was the leader, she had to work out her own destiny first.

Once she had a skeleton plan in place, she called down to the front desk to reserve the rooftop garden for the hour before dawn. Then she called each of her proposed key team members, asking them to meet. She wanted to do this before their flight left.

She didn't explain herself to any of them on the phone, not even Reb. They needed to hear it together, or that defeated the purpose of a team. Reb was curious, but didn't press.

She honored him for that, and loved him just a little more.

Oh, God. Did she love him?

*   *   *

Just before dawn, Elizabeth went to wait on the rooftop. One by one, the men came from the exit hut—Rolex, Exetor Senior, and Reb.

He was as gorgeous as always—no, more gorgeous to her since she'd shared his bed. But as he came onto the roof, his glance at her was wary, and she remembered how she'd left him hanging. Despite that, he managed an encouraging little smile, and she knew he was utterly worth it, and that however hard convincing them might be, it was worth trying for her plan.

"Thanks for joining me." She waved at a tray of go-cups sitting on a wrought iron table. "I got you all coffee."

"Why are we here? You going to axe us, too?" Exetor Senior's demeanor was gruff, but when he plucked his cup from the tray, his hand trembled.

"Last night proved I can run the board with an iron fist. But frankly, that style is going the way of the dinosaur. I'd rather we work together, like when we helped build that house."

"And you'll be the leader," Rolex drawled, but not with his usual condescending sneer.

"Sometimes. Now, yes. After we're up and running, I'll be the heart of the team, most of the time. We'll be flexible around our roles. We need to focus on, not what Lovless Industries was, but who *we'll* be. A better board, stronger together."

"My role?" Reb asked.

This was it. The moment that would make or break them. "Landon Lovless III, as majority owner, you will be the head—most of the time."

"And if I want to return to my SEAL team?" he asked mildly.

"You are, of course, free to go, and if you do, we'll work things out." She knew they'd all be hard sells, but she hadn't thought he'd be the one to object. Had she hurt him, leaving his bed last night? Her heart quailed. God, then it was even more important to convince him to stay, so she could make it up to him. "But I'm hoping we can be your new team." She let her heart show in her gaze. "I hope you'll stay." *With me.*

His eyes widened. "Elizabeth—"

"What will the rest of us do, 'most of the time?'" Senior asked.

She forced her attention from Reb, the hardest thing she'd done yet. She personally needed him for so much more than leading them. But Landy's charities needed all three, equally.

"Roland Exetor Senior. You'll be the brains of the outfit. Map the day-to-day and month-to-month strategies."

"CEO, then." He pushed his lips out thoughtfully, nodding.

"And my role?" Rolex said.

"Roland Exetor Junior—you'll be the hands. Figure out ways to execute the strategies."

"Tactics." Rolex frowned at her. "Like a COO."

"It's absurd," Senior noted. "The board will fight us tooth and nail."

"Then we'll come back out here and build another home, and another, until they understand what's really worth fighting for." She looked hopefully around at the closed faces.

Rolex took an actual step back.

Damn it. "So, what do you all say?" Heart beating painfully in her breast, she held out her hand, palm up. "Will you do it?"

A beat. Two.

Then Reb stepped forward. "I'm in." He put his palm on hers.

Relief and love burst in her breast. *He's with me.* Tempered by, *But the others?* She looked to Senior.

He raised a silver brow. "Just us four?"

"To start. Maybe we can bring in more people later."

"Even your ex?"

Reb said, "He'll have to stop being such a dick."

Elizabeth nearly laughed out loud. "I've heard nearly dying can change a person's whole perspective. Maybe we need to drop a piano on him."

Senior actually chuckled. "What the hell. I'm retiring in a couple years anyway. Might as well go out with a bang." He slapped his hand down on top of Reb's.

Hope soared in her breast. Almost immediately she tempered it by looking at her last, hardest sell. Rolex. Without him, they were like a computer without a keyboard. This all fell apart. "Roland Exetor Junior, will you join us?" She willed him to put his hand on theirs.

Instead, his face screwed up in a horrific grimace. Her heart plummeted.

"Ro-land Ex-e-tor Jun-ior?" he sneered with his old scathing fire. "By the time you get that mouthful out, a falling piano will have shattered my skull."

Hope was a hard beat of her heart.

"Use the name the kids in the hospital gave me." He set down his coffee and slapped his hand on top of his father's. "Call me Tor."

*　　*　　*

The limousines to whisk the Lovless Industries board to the airport waited at the curb, but the members stood motionless, rapt attention on Reb.

Elizabeth stood side by side with her new team, pride surging in her breast as he made the announcement. He was a natural leader. Yes, she'd birthed the team and would be called to run it from time to time. But it was wondrous seeing Reb in a role he was made for.

He finished to a round of enthusiastic applause. The young bucks glowed with possibility, and the hatchet men were nodding. Even the old guard looked less grumpy than usual.

The members, chatting in clumps, boarded the limos. Exetor Senior and Junior—scratch that, Tor—joined them.

Elizabeth lingered, basking in the feeling of accomplishment. Reb stayed by her side.

"That was particularly well done," he said. "Your solution is even better than mine."

"Mine built on yours. I'm pretty chuffed, too, though. Only one thing."

"Oh?"

"Yes. We're on a tropical island paradise—and we haven't gotten to swim in the ocean by moonlight." She turned to him, picturing him nearly naked, his skin sheened with water and kissed by the moon...they'd definitely make love. Her whole body went up in flames.

He laughed. "Tell you what. Next weekend, we'll fly out here for an overnight. That can be our reward for trying to make this work."

Giddy at the idea, she exclaimed, "Rebel Lovless, I love you."

Almost immediately she realized what she'd done. *Too fast, Rothschild.* "I mean—"

"Hey." He turned to her, took both hands in his, and swung them playfully. "I love you, too." The softness in his eyes made her own well with happiness.

They were about to wage an uphill battle. Duty to a dying old man would've made her struggle as best she could, but the thought of battling alongside Reb, then rewarding herself with a weekend with him, almost made her look forward to fight.

*   *   *

Two months later, Elizabeth was on her way to another Lovless Industries board meeting. But there were welcome

123

differences—no muggings, and she'd left Fido happily gnawing at his catnip mouse.

The boardroom doors were still as heavy and imposing. But beyond them, the long table with its power positions had been replaced with a round, central table and several work areas along the walls where members could cluster and brainstorm.

Instead of churning fear and anticipating a ring of moneyed, entitled men, contempt glittering in their eyes, she looked forward to seeing these men—and a few new women—who she'd begun to call friends.

And one more change. The most important. Instead of facing the boardroom doors alone, she held the hand of one of the strongest men she knew. She'd helped him make peace with his grandfather's ghost, and in turn, he'd not only retired from active duty, he'd dedicated himself to continuing his grandfather's charities and helping her take Lovless Industries into the future.

He'd given her his protection, his aid, and his heart.

She squeezed her fingers around his.

Reb smiled down at her. "Ready to do this?"

She smiled back. "Ready."

In a symbol of unity that filled her with contentment and pride, she opened one boardroom door as he flung open the other. In perfect synch as always, they strode in together.

Continue reading for the first chapter from Hot Chips and Sand.

About the Author

Mary Hughes (written Hug-he's but possibly pronounced throat warbler mangrove) writes smart and sassy stories of action and love.

She's a bona fide computer geek and performing flutist. (And piccolo, but we don't talk about that.) When this USA Today Bestselling Author isn't busy finding the missing </> tag or blowing her lungs out, she's on the couch reading or binging on The Flash, Elementary, NCIS, or Wynonna Earp...and petting the cats that inevitably end up on her lap.

Mary's online and would love to hear from you!
Newsletter http://www.maryhughesbooks.com/Newsletter.html
Facebook http://www.facebook.com/MaryHughesAuthor
Twitter http://www.twitter.com/MaryHughesBooks
Instagram https://www.instagram.com/maryhughesbooks
BookBub https://www.bookbub.com/authors/mary-hughes
Goodreads
http://www.goodreads.com/author/show/279140.Mary_Hughes
Website http://www.maryhughesbooks.com/
Blog http://maryhughesbooks.blogspot.com/

Hot Chips and Sand
© 2016 Mary Hughes

When American Skyler Jones is kidnapped, she manages a heart-pounding escape, only to be cornered in the hotel room of a lithe, enigmatic man. The kidnappers burst into the room, but the man hides Skyler by covering her body with his—and kissing her. Her kidnappers are thrown long enough for the man, known only as Cliff, to race Skyler through narrow streets and hide her on a boat going home.

Skyler thinks her troubles are over, but Cliff is really Sir Humphrey Hawkesclyffe, genius inventor of the next gen supercomputer. He's zeroed in on Skyler—he says for heading his software development team, business only. But as they work together, Skyler starts to fall for the lonely boy genius who's become a rugged man of action.

He seems to fall for her, too—at least their sizzling kisses suggest more than simple chemistry. But is Cliff just mixing pleasure with his business? And then the kidnappers come back for round two...but it's not Skyler they've come for this time.

Enjoy the following chapter from Hot Chips and Sand:

Skyler Jones was deep into coding a project her boss had shoved onto her last minute yesterday, due in two hours. She'd gotten her teeth into it and was thinking she might actually pull off a miracle and get it done, when said boss appeared in the opening of her cubicle like *Office Space*'s version of a grim reaper.

"Drop everything, Skyler. We have a new client." Phil Westerby smacked a letter on Skyler's desk. He cheerfully acknowledged his beer belly and three-hair comb-over was less a graceful slide toward middle age and more stealing the base. But his management style was all *Art of War.* "Rush-rush."

"They're all rush-rush." Skyler turned from her computer screen to give her boss her full attention. "You know I have at least three projects due this week, right? Including the one you gave me yesterday."

"Colonel Fahrrad takes priority." Phil thumped the letter in underscore. "Potential international client. Could be big money."

Irritation ruffled Skyler's nerves, the curse of a redhead's temper. Not that she bought into the stereotype, but she was a redhead, and she did have a temper. "Naturally, you'll forgive any of my missed deadlines."

"Would a little overtime hurt you? Besides, this is for a security system, the kind of project you love."

She stifled a sigh. Normally she did love her job at Fitzwater Software and Consulting. It was the perfect combination of meeting new people and problem solving. And she *wanted* to be helpful. "All right, let me take a look."

She lifted the paper. Good quality, with dented print like an impact printer or a real typewriter instead of a laptop and inkjet. Possibly the client had a secretary who simply loved the feel of an old-fashioned typebar, but more likely a client helplessly mired in the last century.

Reading the letter, she started getting a whole lot of bad vibes. "This Colonel Fahrrad already contracted with another vendor. Do you think the other vendor knows he's sniffing out the competition?"

"Sure. I think. Probably. Does it matter?"

"That he might be going behind the vendor's back?" A wave of annoyance made her clench her teeth. Like the high school guy who brought a girl to a dance, then left her alone so he could chat up other girls. Or fiancés who'd test-drive other models before he even got a woman off the showroom lot. Not that she had experience of that. Much. "Yes. I have to ask how serious this guy really is."

"Serious enough that I scheduled you to meet him today at two."

"The conference room is booked—"

"Boardroom."

That stopped her. Usually only upper management used the boardroom. "You must really want this client."

"The company president does. International, Skyler."

"That's nice." She pushed the letter back across the desk at him. "But I don't think I'm right for this."

"You know what I think? I think you have an appointment at two." He gave the letter one final thump and stalked away.

She closed her eyes for a moment to get her frustration under control. She prided herself on being professional, but sometimes, like now, it was hard.

Deep inhale. Breathe frustration out. Five of those and she felt calm enough to open her eyes. Time to do a little research on the colonel. She pulled up a browser and abruptly lost all the calm she'd fought for.

Boris Fahrrad had been secret police back when the KGB was cool. He'd been run out of several countries for archaic interrogation techniques.

In February of this year, he'd been hired by a progressive Middle East prince to help stabilize the small country of Middle Yemen.

Then, on the first day of June, Fahrrad staged a coup.

She sucked in a breath. That sure as heck explained the desire for a palace security system. He'd want to make sure no one would pull the same trick on him.

Checking dates, she saw that was only a week ago. This guy was a real winner, kicking out the old regime then off on a shopping spree within days.

Despite her churning gut, she put the two p.m. appointment in her calendar. Fitzwater had given her a job at her lowest point. Her loyalty couldn't be bought, but it could be won. If Jerry Fitzwater wanted this contract, she'd do everything she could to secure it, including meeting a scary dictator dude.

Besides, this was her job. While at one point, she'd dreamed of having it all, having a balanced life—a nice job, a nice family, even a nice house with a white picket fence— her fiancé had screwed that over when he screwed *her* over. Her career was all she had left.

She was very serious about her career.

Breathe in, push pain out. Turning from the deep pang of memory, she set her mind to finishing rush-rush project number two and clear the deck for the new number one.

A few moments later, her calendar chimed. She looked up, disoriented. She'd been deep in her work.

"Two p.m. boardroom" blinked on her screen.

"Two, already?" Panic goosed her to grab her phone and a client welcome folder then dash to the boardroom. She threw open the door to meet Colonel Fahrrad.

Seated at the long, glossy table was a slight man with a toothbrush mustache wearing an over-designed uniform and too-big hat. His beady eyes were glued to a sales brochure before him.

Her first impression was Classic Dictator ala *Mission Impossible.*

"Two-oh-one. You're late." He spoke without looking up. "Mr. Jones, the president told me you were the very best your company has to offer, but this tardiness does not speak well." His gaze rose. And stopped, shocked. "*Ms.* Jones."

As she introduced herself, he sat transfixed, gaze avid on her.

Because he was expecting a man, or did she have lunch salad in her teeth? She sat cautiously beside him.

"What an unusual color for hair." He reached out and grabbed a curl.

Alarm spiked her. She automatically swatted the strand from his grip.

His eyes sparked with thwarted anger. But he controlled himself, and actually smiled, with a toothy, gold-capped grin and a slight nod in apology.

Fighting to keep her professionalism, she began, "Your letter said you wanted a security system, Colonel Fahrrad. But you're already working with another company—"

"My predecessor's choice, sweeting. I wish to make my own alliances."

That actually made sense, but the endearment grated. She tried again. "Fitzwater doesn't do hardware, though. We specialize in database design and implementation."

"I am not worried about hardware, sweeting. Or anything hard." His slow, sensual grin sent frissons of unease up her spine.

If he hadn't been a potential client—scratch that, a potential *international* client, deeply desired by the president of the company—she'd have walked out. As it was, she asked politely, "What do you want the security system for? Your government headquarters?"

"For the entire country."

"Wh-what?" Surprise drove the word from her lips. "The technology for securing a bank or building exists, but a whole country...? Wouldn't your military be a better bet?"

"Middle Yemen is too small and too poor, sweeting. But *you* have exactly what I need." Again that oily grin.

Actual alarm goosed Skyler to her feet. She suppressed a shudder to slide him the welcome folder. "Tell you what. Have your people send us the specs, and we'll get you a quote. My card's in the pocket. Thank you for your time. I'll have someone show you out." She scrambled out of there and hoped never to see Fahrrad again.

Two days later, as she left work late, she was kidnapped.

Four men came out of the blue and plucked her right off the Boston sidewalk. Shock stunned her long enough for them to slide her toward the open back door of a black sedan. *If they get me in there, I may never return.* The dark maw disturbed her enough that she began to struggle. She wriggled loose and ran back toward the building but only got three steps before they caught her. Freaked, she did the first thing she thought of—she chucked her messenger bag into the nearest bush. She hoped someone would find it and know she was in trouble.

They stuffed her in the car. One held a out blindfold—and a gun. He didn't say a word, but the muzzle spoke for him quite clearly. She put the blindfold on.

Without sight, she got a skewed sense of time and place. Car ride. Being hustled through open space up a set of stairs. Sensation of intense speed and dropping stomach. Airplane? The drone of engine went on and on. With each passing moment her body got colder, and her mind floated farther away.

The riffle of cards. Her kidnappers broke their silence over what sounded like a card game. She didn't recognize any of the words, though.

Except one—Fahrrad.

That sent her stomach into shut-down mode.

Two stops. Three times she smelled food. Somewhere between twenty and thirty hours later, a door *shooshed* open, and she was pushed onto her wobbling legs into a wall of heat.

Her whole body went from ice to ash, no thawing in between. Trembling badly, she stumbled down clanging stairs onto tarmac so gooey it stuck to her shoes as she tried to walk. The air smelled of sand and spices and was so hot it hurt to breathe.

In the small, sane corner of her mind where she huddled, she remembered the saying "It's not the heat, it's the humidity."

Her lungs burning from the inside out, she thought, *No, it's definitely the heat.*

They removed her blindfold in a dank, sweltering room. Bed, small table, attached bath...it looked like a run-down hotel room.

One of the men shoved a dark blotch at her. But she only stared at it, hollow inside. Terror must've burned her out.

The goon shook the thing at her and spat some angry-sounding words. The blotch resolved as her eyes adjusted to a red teddy, mostly lace and air. Familiar.

Like the one she'd bought for her wedding night.

The guy shook the teddy again then pointed at her—with a gun.

In the hollow of her chest, anger sparked. She'd been harassed, kidnapped, threatened, and now was being rudely forced to wear an article of clothing she'd sworn never to put on for a man again.

The spark of emotion saved her from breaking down. She fanned her anger and felt a modicum of control return to her limbs. *Damn straight. I'm not gonna let a dictator with a bad hat and his goons get me down.*

Snatching the teddy, she stalked into the room's bathroom, a closet-with-toilet. As she changed, she searched the tiny room. The cabinet behind the mirror yielded a handful of bobby pins that she stuck into her hair—might come in handy for picking a lock, if she knew how to pick a lock. Still, doing something, anything, made her feel better, more in control.

She needed that feeling when she came out and they burned her own clothes.

"Hey, I might need those," she protested.

One had enough English to answer, "Not with the colonel." But they all leered in the international language of *yuck.*

She needed an escape plan.

First chance I get, I'm getting out of here.

As plans went, it was short on details. But her ears perked when one of the kidnappers patted his growling stomach. The wiry bilingual leader nodded, pointed at her, and barked a command at the smallest kidnapper, a thin youth barely past pimples. The youth scowled as the leader and the other two swaggered out.

Going out for dinner to celebrate, no doubt, leaving Scowly behind to guard her.

She gauged the kid's physique. Stringy but underfed. She probably outweighed him by ten pounds and had at least a couple inches on him.

She could take him. All she had to do was judge her moment.

Then Scowly cut considering eyes to her, licking his chops in a way that made her shudder. *Oh, no.* She crossed her arms over her breasts and mentally promised him dismemberment if he tried. *I'll fight. You may win, but not before I take thirty-five cents of your best hamburger.*

He growled but picked up a magazine.

Pressing a hand to her breastbone, she was surprised to feel her heart thudding hard and fast. That wouldn't help. She coached herself. *Deep breath in, press stress out.* Wait for the right moment.

She fisted hands and waited. And waited. She was ready to scream when her captor pointed to her and barked a word, probably "Stay," because he went into the bathroom and shut the door.

Yes. While he was relieving himself, she quietly let herself out.

She found herself in a narrow, airless corridor lined by doors. Definitely a hotel or boarding house. To her right, the corridor ended in a wall. To her left, it ended in a door.

Picking the door direction, heart pounding, she ran.

The door opened to a narrow, airless stairwell, hot as a chimney. Wood stairs. If anything had told her she wasn't in the USA anymore, Toto, those rickety wooden stairs were it. She crept down, panting heat like sandpaper, trying not to get splinters in her bare feet.

A switchback flight emptied into a well with *two* doors. The one before her probably led to another dank corridor. Swallowing dry, hot air, she chose the one behind.

It opened onto a lobby. Her heart soared. A lobby meant an exit, people, maybe even a police force. She took a couple steps into the room. Wall cubbies were stuffed with mail. A couple rickety chairs sat on cracked linoleum.

The door shut behind her, revealing a large curled-up orange triangle in the corner. Modern sculpture? She stopped for a moment, trying to calm her frightened panting, and stared at the bizarre art sitting mid-dirt.

The outside door banged open. The three kidnappers returned just then, bearing bags wafting spicy odors. Carryout.

Heart nearly exploding from her chest, she scoured the room for a place to hide, but the rickety furniture wouldn't conceal a praying mantis, much less her.

She spun and took to the stairs.

Adrenaline rocketed her up a half-flight before the searing heat leached all the strength from her. Legs stuttering, she forced herself to trot up the second half-flight to the original floor, ears straining for shouts of discovery and a slammed door below.

Nothing.

Passing the landing, a stitch grabbed her ribs as she started up the next half flight, slowing her to a limping walk.

This was not good. Her mind screamed at her to run, but her body screamed at her to slow down, rest. The hours of sitting, the terror, the killing heat, had eaten away most of her strength, and that panicked run had drained what was left.

Palm on the wall, she stopped mid-flight to bend over, panting. "I am strong," she told herself firmly. "I work out. I am reasonably healthy. And above all, I am *not* panicking..."

A shout from downstairs made her heart skip.

She started leaping steps two at a time. Cracked plaster walls flew by. She tried to remember her pep talk.

Not panicking. So what if kidnappers are chasing me? It's no worse than Phil hounding me for his TPS reports. An absurd image of her boss, his spindly arms toting a gun Rambo-style as he demanded his reports, distracted her from the growing stitch in her side. But the pain grew until she thought she had a burst appendix.

Pausing on the third floor landing, she held her cramped side, puffing breath. "I am strong," she coached herself. "I work out. *But not in hundred-degree heat.* "Definitely reconsidering...the all...Cheez Curlz diet."

Bam-bam.

Skyler froze, all her muscles clenched as she strained to identify the sound.

Thudding, rhythmic. Feet, hitting the stairs below. Damn it, her opportunity to escape, blown sky-high. Well, what did she expect, with her elaborate plan consisting of R, U, and N?

Hiding place. Panic goosed her to leap up stairs to the fourth floor landing.

Where the stairs ran out.

"Fry my motherboard." She scanned the small space. A ladder hung from the wall, and a hatch perforated the ceiling. Grabbing the ladder, she nearly beaned herself pulling it down. Lug the ladder into position, climb it with her trembling limbs, all before the kidnappers caught her?

Not happening.

She spun and ran back down the stairs. She'd made the second floor landing—just as the door flew open.

Throwing herself behind it with raised hands, she suffered a whack to her shielding forearms. As the door swung closed, she saw the legs of two kidnappers running up the stairs. Heads indicated two were running down.

Arms smarting, stomach churning, she followed the legs as the lesser of two evils. They turned past the third floor, continuing up. She followed cautiously. Peeked around the switch just in time to see one pair of feet disappear through the fourth-floor door—while the other stood guard.

Searching top to bottom while the other pair searched bottom to top? And they'd meet like a pair of clapping hands in the middle, trapping her.

Still, what choice did she have? She tiptoed back to the third floor landing. Panting, she cracked the door.

A dungeon corridor stretched before her, even danker than the second floor. It appeared carpeted in a sluggish river of blood and walled with a corpse's teeth.

She blinked. Her eyes adjusted to the low watt bulbs, and the hallway resolved to a dirty floor with a ratty red runner and chewed plaster walls picketed by narrow wooden doors. None of the teeth—er, doors—shouted, "Hide here."

Fighting to control her thudding heart and trembling limbs, she slid through the door into the hallway. Her mind clicked through and discarded possibilities as fast as a multicore processor. Open closed doors, possibly meet more goons.

Run back downstairs, *definitely* meet the kidnappers.

If only this were a computer game. A save game would be nice about now. Or a pause button. Why didn't life have a pause? Then she could try each of those doors, restoring each time one opened to a monster.

But no. If she screwed up, it'd be *Game Over*. Her stomach knotted.

Shouting. Footsteps on the stairs pounded down. She glanced back at the stairwell door, her throat tightening.

Hide. Didn't matter what might be behind the room doors, she definitely knew what was flying toward her in the stairwell. With a deep breath for courage, she scurried to the first door on the left and cranked the yellowed glass knob.

Locked.

"Smack me with a Dell." Rattling the knob did no good, nor did kicking the door, which, since her feet were bare, stung her toes. She hopped around, trying to bring the pain under control, remembered *Game Over,* and hobbled across the narrow hallway to grab a second door knob. She turned and pushed.

It gave.

She half-ran, half-fell into the room, slamming the door closed behind her, her chest heaving with relief.

Hiding place. Skyler scanned the room—and froze.

Standing mid-room was a giant.

Half-naked. Sun-bronzed chest. Very, very male.

And staring at her with eyes so blue they were pure cobalt fire.

www.ingramcontent.com/pod-product-compliance
Lightning Source LLC
Chambersburg PA
CBHW060746210726
48292CB00015B/2809